Helen Brent, M.D.

Helen Brent, M.D.

A Social Study

Annie Nathan Meyer

Introduction by

Stephanie Peebles Tavera

Hastings College Press | Hastings, Nebraska

Introduction © 2020 by Hastings College Press

Text © 1892 by Cassell Publishing Company. This book has fallen into the public domain and is no longer subject to copyright protection.

Production Staff

Makayla Baker	Alexandria Kreikemeier
Emilie Barnes	Gabrielle Rodgers
Megan Beirow	Makenzie Shofner
Jordan Brown	Carly Spotts-Falzone
Nicole Chavez	Jeri Thompson
Natalee Hanway	Kimberly Villanueva
Nicole Havlik	Anna Weber

ISBN-10: 194288558X
ISBN-13: 978-1-942885-58-0

Note on the text: This edition has been reset from the first (1892) edition. Original spelling and grammatical conventions have been maintained, except in the case of publishing errors in the first edition. The original punctuation has been maintained but updated using modern conventions (e.g., eliminating spaces around dashes).

Contents

Introduction

Stephanie Peebles Tavera

Historians often remember Annie Nathan Meyer for her role in
founding Barnard College, one of the Seven Sisters institutions that
was among the first to grant women college degrees.[1] However,
Meyer was also a prolific writer. During her career, Meyer wrote
no less than thirty plays; sixty-three short stories, essays, and
sketches published in periodicals; three novels; three memoirs
(including an autobiography); three non-fiction guides, including
My Park Book and *The Gallery-Goers Book;* and an edited collection
of feminist essays, entitled *Women's Work in America*. She also
kept diaries throughout her life and wrote hundreds of letters,
including daily notes to her beloved husband, Alfred Meyer. She is
not often remembered as a professional writer or playwright. Nor
does she frequently appear in the American literary canon, literary

---

[1] Meyer is perhaps better remembered because of the debate surrounding
her role as Barnard founder. As Lynn D. Gordon explains, the history
books *reluctantly* remember Annie Nathan Meyer as a founder of Barnard
College, giving most of the credit to Barnard's first dean, Virginia C.
Gildersleeve. Gordon cites a number of reasons for this discrepancy in the
historical record, all of which relate to constructing an appropriate image
for Barnard's founder: Meyer "did not symbolize its mission or vision" as
she did not graduate from college herself, held "anachronistic" feminist
perspectives that did not agree with mainstream feminism, and was Jewish,
which was an "undesirable" trait for the founder of Barnard College (508).

scholarship, or in American literature courses, as do her role models Margaret Fuller and Edith Wharton.[2]

Meyer always hoped to be a writer. In a diary entry dated December 26, 1890, Meyer remarks that she is "rewriting 'Problems,'" her first novel, which would be published as *Helen Brent, M.D.* (1892). She states that she "hopes to have it ready for publication within a year," but worries whether her novel—and she as a writer—will amount to anything: "That is the great question that bothers me just now. *Will I, do I* amount to anything in a literary way" (Diary). It is a question, she states, that makes her "frequently miserable" (Diary). Her novels sold only moderately well, and her plays were granted limited showings. Thus, like many writers, during her life Meyer had little success, but she has the potential for greater success and appreciation posthumously.

In her autobiography, *It's Been Fun* (1951), Meyer attributes her limited success to timeliness. She was "ahead of [her] time," she admits of her work in general (3). Speaking specifically of her first novel, *Helen Brent, M.D.*, Meyer recalls:

> *Helen Brent, M.D.* came out anonymously (Cassell) in 1893. Because it was the story of a woman who refused to give up her career for marriage, the author was assumed to be a sour old maid. I remember with what glee Jeanette Gilder announced that it was written

---

[2] Meyer frequently references Margaret Fuller in her published work and in her diaries. In *Helen Brent, M.D.*, Meyer draws on Fuller's theories of sex from "Woman in the Nineteenth Century" (54), which Lotus is also seen reading (59). Meyer also admired Edith Wharton, whom she once met for lunch, according to a diary entry dated May 2, 1902.

by a young and happily married woman. But it was
ahead of its day; for it handled with great frankness the
theme of social evil. (*It's Been Fun* 218)

Many of her contemporary critics and present-day scholars
have summarized Meyer's *Helen Brent, M.D.* in a similar manner,
reducing its plot to a simple "marriage-or-career" narrative
characteristic of late nineteenth-century lady-doctor novels.
Yet, Meyer explicitly states her theme addressed "social evil," a
metonymic phrase used in the late nineteenth-century for venereal
disease and prostitution.

Placed within the context of feminism and social reform
movements from the 1890s, Meyer's novel appears far more than
a simple reflection of the professional woman's social struggles
at the *fin de siècle*. In addressing the theme of "social evil," *Helen
Brent, M.D.* offers an argument for social reform on behalf of the
social purity movement, a *fin de siècle* health reform movement
that sought to eradicate venereal disease and prostitution. The
social purity movement itself was not feminist. Meyer, however,
approaches her theme from a feminist perspective, since during the
nineteenth century, women's bodies were frequently pathologized as
"diseased," an assumption she seeks to disprove.[3]

---

[3] Prior to the 1890s, most medical authorities agreed that women carried
"some taint of venereal disease" (Spongberg 6). This assumption, however,
did not differentiate between the upright woman and the fallen woman.
The former included wives and mothers whose specific role was to provide
a model for moral behavior for their husbands and children. The latter
predominately referred to prostitutes. Since the upright woman could not
be considered simultaneously "diseased" and moral, by the *fin de siècle*, the
body of the prostitute alone became pathologized as the "diseased woman"

Many of Meyer's works were what her editor at Cassell
Publishing Company, Jeanette Gilder, called "stories with a
purpose." They contributed a socially relevant message for readers
and often warned against certain practices, even calling for reform
or proposing specific reform measures. In a letter dated March 29,
1892, Gilder not only refers to Meyer's novel as a "story with a
purpose" but also persuades Meyer to retitle her novel from *Problems*
to *Helen Brent, M.D.* so as to minimize her intent:

> I am very much afraid that you would defeat your
> object—so far as my reading public is concerned, if
> you labeled your series "Problems" ... Stories with
> a purpose are not branded as such in their titles. If
> you call your book "Helen Brent, M.D.," which is Mr.
> Wagstaff's choice, you pique curiosity and attract
> attention at once, if you give away its purpose on the
> cover you frighten off just those whom you wish to
> catch. Let the reader discover the purpose.

Today, scholars refer to "stories with a purpose" as political fiction
or social reform fiction, both of which derived from realism.[4] Like

---

responsible for spreading syphilis and gonorrhea. Meyer does not explicitly
address prostitution or the body of the prostitute in *Helen Brent, M.D.*, but
she does challenge the "diseased woman" narrative in general.

[4] Donald Pizer offers, perhaps, the most comprehensive definition of
literary realism and the realist movement. Although he agrees that realist
fiction seeks to document "the commonplace," Pizer also finds that realist
fiction represents the protagonist's relationship with his/her particular
social world. Often this relationship introduces a moral tension or
conflict, and within that tension, "formalized codes of social behavior and

Harriet Beecher Stowe's *Uncle Tom's Cabin* (1852), which was
an early example of the genre in the American literary tradition,
authors of political reform novels seek "active reform driven by the
presentation of empirical evidence and a commitment to curing
some class-free, focused social ill" (Rhodes 188). In the case of
Meyer's *Helen Brent, M.D.*, the "focused social ill" is reproductive
rights, or perhaps more specifically, a woman's right to social
hygiene education, or sex education, and not just simply a woman's
right to a professional career. Meyer presents "empirical evidence"
through the eyes of her protagonist, Dr. Helen Brent, whose
patients and their medical cases offer support for her social reform
argument.

The Birth of Helen Brent, M.D.

Annie Nathan Meyer was born in New York City on February 19,
1867, to a Sephardic Jewish family. The youngest daughter of
Annie Florence Nathan (d. 1878) and Robert Weeks Nathan (d.
1888), Meyer was born to privilege. The Nathans were prominent
members of the community, and especially the New York City
elite. Meyer's scrapbook contains numerous newspaper clippings
documenting their activities such as weddings, births, or high-
profile events. Meyer spent her entire life in New York City, save

---

belief" are reimagined. Realist fiction does not represent this relationship
objectively, rather Pizer finds it highly subjective in that realist authors
often present their own answers to moral and ethical dilemmas through
their fictional characters. Political fiction, social reform fiction, and even
medical fiction derive from realism in their response to contemporaneous
social issues that the author not only seeks to represent realistically but also
to propose real-world solutions to through his/her characters.

for a brief period during her childhood following the stock market crash of 1875. The family moved to Green Bay, Wisconsin, until Annie Florence Nathan's death in 1878, upon which Annie Nathan Meyer, her father, two brothers, and sister permanently returned to New York City. Although Meyer traveled extensively during her life, and especially her later years, she would always consider New York City her home. "New York is in my blood," she writes in her autobiography. "Eight generations in my family have been born here. I feel as though I have lived here all my life," and essentially, she had, with the exception of four years in the Midwest (*It's Been Fun* 93).

Meyer lived in New York City during a period in which the urban center became a site for feminist reform and the leading center for gynecology. These developing communities frequently intersected, since J. Marion Sims, the "father of gynecology," established his Woman's Hospital in New York City in 1855. By the 1890s, Sims's hospital had developed a reputation for its role in gynecological research and as a training ground for recent medical school graduates. It also provided an impetus for health reformers like Annie Nathan Meyer in proving a need for social hygiene education, or sex education. Like his contemporaries, J. Marion Sims believed in what Ben Barker-Benfield refers to as "gynecologic materialism," or the prevailing belief among nineteenth-century medical practitioners that women were defined by their uterus and ovaries (279). This definition identified women's unique sexual organs and their role in reproduction as responsible for her frail constitution (Haller and Haller 37). In other words, the very fact a woman has monthly menses defines her as not only weaker, but also incapable of performing mental and physical activities such as studying or bicycle-riding equal with her male counterpart.

Women, and especially feminist social reformers, found
their disenfranchisement rooted in medicine, or gynecologic
materialism. They therefore concluded that the solution must also
be found in reforming medical practices. For this reason, John S.
Haller and Robin M. Haller find the early feminist movement
developed alongside the field of gynecology (41, xii). Annie Nathan
Meyer's life and career confirm Haller and Haller's hypothesis,
since Meyer faced this disenfranchisement rooted in gynecologic
materialism head-on when she attended the Collegiate Course for
Women at Columbia University. In 1883, Columbia University
first offered a Collegiate Course for Women after a group of
prominent New Yorkers repeatedly petitioned for women's access to
higher education (Gordon 504). Meyer discovered in attending this
course that higher education standards for women were certainly
not equal to those for men. After each course, which consisted of
no more than two conferences with the instructor, female students
could sit for final examinations. Should those female students pass
a sufficient number of examinations, they could receive a bachelor's
degree from Columbia University. However, the professors who
created and proctored these examinations based their questions
upon lectures given in their courses, and female students were not
permitted to attend those courses (Gordon 504). Meyer recalls her
experience in *It's Been Fun*:

> Here was I, who had been endeavoring to become an
> honor and an example to the rest of my sex—staring
> hopelessly at my very first examination paper! Was I,
> then, to flunk what hosts of boys would pass? Perish
> the thought! Getting a grip on myself, I answered such
> questions as I understood and then coolly wrote in

the examination paper that certain of the questions
evidently referred to the professor's lectures, which I
had not been privileged to hear. (159)

The professor ultimately passed Meyer, perhaps for her acute
sense of justice—or her snark. She would not, however, continue
in the program. Meyer dropped out of the Collegiate Course for
Women in 1887, the same year that she married Dr. Alfred Meyer,
a pulmonologist and specialist in the study of tuberculosis.

Meyer understood and empathized with women's struggle in
achieving higher education, and because women's access to higher
education was intimately connected with nineteenth-century
gynecological theory and practice, she recognized her political
arguments must draw on medical authority. Annie Nathan married
Dr. Alfred Meyer on February 15, 1887, an event that profoundly
influenced her politics and writing. Alfred Meyer was himself a
health reformer in his New York City community, advocating for
street cleaning, improved sanitary methods, and health education
in prevention of tuberculosis (Goldenberg 147–48, n57). He also
successfully reformed nurses' training at Mount Sinai Hospital,
where he was employed as a pulmonologist. Meyer often joined
her husband in his reform endeavors, and even once lectured at
Mount Sinai Hospital's Nurses Training School upon her husband's
request (Goldenberg 147, n57). Her scrapbooks contain numerous
clippings from articles on nurses' training, advances in medicine,
and debates within the medical community. She was well-informed
in the field of medicine and developed strong opinions on medical
ethics (Gordon 508).

During this period, Meyer was also seeped in feminist
activism, specifically women's access to higher education. She

became a leader among prominent New Yorkers who envisioned an annex similar to Harvard University's Harvard Annex (which would become Radcliffe College in 1894), where women could earn collegiate degrees equal to men (Gordon 504). Even before leaving the Collegiate Course for Women, Meyer rallied support for a new women's college associated with Columbia University. She petitioned Columbia trustees for support, persuaded prominent New Yorkers to donate funds for the cause, and publicized the new college by writing and publishing articles in influential New York publications. In 1889, Barnard College opened its doors at a brownstone house at 343 Madison Avenue. Twelve years later, in 1897, funds were raised for construction of a new campus at Morningside Heights (Gordon 505). Meyer would serve as a trustee for Barnard College until her death in 1951, and she even financially sponsored Barnard's first black student, author Zora Neale Hurston (Gordon 505, 517).

In the same years that Meyer petitioned for Barnard College, she edited *Women's Work in America* (1891), a collection of essays on women's public social roles and social work. Contributors to the collection include feminist writers and activists Julie Ward Howe, Frances E. Willard, Dr. Mary Putnam Jacobi, and Clara Barton. Meyer also began writing *Helen Brent, M.D.* during these years, in fact, as early as 1890, according to a diary entry dated September 7, 1890. Her public activist work in women's rights and health reform merge in her writing of *Helen Brent, M.D.*, as they did in New York City social reform at large. As Meyer reminisces on her husband's work in *It's Been Fun*, "[Alfred] had more to do with developing a consciousness of tuberculosis as a social disease than any one man" in New York (140). He founded the movement for State and City Sanatoria, and exposed tuberculosis as a social disease not connected with race or class, but one's living conditions. In *Helen Brent, M.D.*, Meyer articulates a similar truth, namely that venereal diseases such as syphilis and gonorrhea are also social diseases not originating from "woman," but instead develop in any individual regardless of sex or gender as a result of poor sex education. Meyer's scrapbook further reveals her familiarity with the Woman's Hospital and its founders, which likely influenced her writing of *Helen Brent M.D.* and its political message. Her scrapbook contains an article on T. Gaillard Thomas, a well-known gynecologist during the nineteenth century, and a protégé and colleague of J. Marion Sims. Thomas worked at the Woman's Hospital in New York and was the first doctor to perform and publish an account on vaginal ovariotomy (in 1870).

Meyer likely draws on her knowledge of T. Gaillard Thomas in critiquing the Woman's Hospital and offering a feminist alternative in her fictionalized Root Memorial Hospital from *Helen Brent, M.D.*. Unlike Sims's Woman's Hospital, the Root Memorial Hospital was established by women: Mrs. Phineas Root, the philanthropist, and Dr. Helen Brent, the founder and manager. At the beginning of the novel, the affluent Mrs. Root awards Dr. Brent the Root Memorial Fund for the establishment of the Root Memorial Hospital and College for Women after Dr. Brent successfully performs a vaginal ovariotomy on Mrs. Root herself. Although it might seem anti-feminist for a woman doctor to perform sexual surgeries on a patient of her own sex, Meyer's narrative choice seeks to establish her credibility as a medical fiction author and her protagonist's credibility as a woman doctor. Neither role was wholly accepted during the *fin de siècle;* therefore, Meyer must do something radical for her period to prove her legitimacy in medical discourse; namely she must acknowledge sexual surgeries.⁵ Once accepted as a member of the medical discourse community, Meyer, using her protagonist Dr. Helen Brent, can successfully prove women's participation in medical practice, especially gynecology, and the need for women's access to sex education. *Helen Brent, M.D.* itself might even be considered a sex education text in that Meyer educates her readers by embedding her own knowledge of gynecology into the narrative itself.

Helen Brent, M.D. is the only work of medical fiction that Annie Nathan Meyer published during her lifetime, though her diaries and her autobiography *It's Been Fun* both suggest that reproductive health remained a concern for Meyer beyond her first novel. In a previously undiscovered journal entry dated October 14, 1922, Meyer exclaims that "a new satire idea—just sprang into [her] head," and she must sketch it out before it escapes her (Diary). She proceeds to outline her novel's basic plot, which eerily parallels earlier radical feminist utopian novels such as Mary E.

---

⁵ J. Marion Sims's research and publications on vesico-vaginal fistulas established sexual surgeries as a primary function in the field of gynecology. Successful performance of sexual surgeries—including cliterodectomy, hysterectomy, and oophorectomy or ovariotomy (also called "female castration")—became the standard by which one's authority was measured in the gynecological community, once the American Gynecological Society was established in 1875. This accounts for why Helen Brent must perform a hysterectomy on Mrs. Phineas Root as a means of (1) establishing credibility in the medical community and (2) gaining financial support for the Root Memorial Hospital and College for Women. Performance of sexual surgeries raises a question of ethics in gynecological theory and practice. Nevertheless, Helen Brent must perform sexual surgeries as a means of establishing authority and gaining a hearing among the medical community, whether she, or Meyer, agree with such practices.

Bradley Lane's *Mizora* (1880–1881) and Charlotte Perkins Gilman's *Herland* (1915): "Years from now women have been so loose and Birth Control has been so much employed that no children are being born at least not enough to carry on with," Meyer narrates. "Something must be done," and so "learned scientists" begin "investigating life," or presumably the origin of life (Diary). Like Lane and Gilman, Meyer's unpublished feminist utopian novel reveals anxieties with reproductive technologies and a complicated approach toward birth control that is simultaneously feminist and eugenic.[6] Her description of an all-female separatist utopia heralds female scientists as the necessary utopian guides for finding a solution to reproductive issues. As her sketch unfolds, Meyer reintroduces men into this all-female separatist utopia. Through her unnamed protagonist, a woman scientist convinces a "big leader among women" to bear children with a man *en vivo*, rather than artificially *en vitro* (Diary). Similar to *Helen Brent, M.D.*, Meyer's sketch delves into advocacy for sex education in her emphasis on teaching women how to reproduce heterosexually.

In her autobiography, Meyer alludes to an unpublished novel "written about thirty-five years ago," circa 1916, "about a woman

---

[6] Jane Carey reveals that birth control has a complicated history, since it emerged from both the early women's rights movement and the eugenics movement. Significant figures from the birth control movement, including Margaret Sanger, Annie Besant, and Marie Stopes, were also eugenicists. Authors of feminist utopian fiction also reveal this intersection, since eugenics and feminist arguments appear in each author's respective texts, among them Mary E. Bradley Lane's *Mizora* (1880–1881), Charlotte Perkins Gilman's *Herland* (1915), and Marion Piddington's *Via Nuova* (1916). This intersection is also reflected in each author's support or activism for the eugenics movement and the feminist movement.

who craved maternity, but who did not want either marriage or just sleeping with a man" (*It's Been Fun* 3). Meyer reveals the theme of this unpublished novel centered on "artificial insemination, a theme which shocked two publishing houses to the marrow" (*It's Been Fun* 3). She did not submit her manuscript further after these rejections, and her novel remains unpublished. Could Meyer be referring to the novel she sketched in her diary entry dated October 14, 1922? Might the narrative have evolved differently than she originally planned? We may never know whether they are one and the same novel. We can, however, surmise that Meyer was not finished with reproductive issues after *Helen Brent, M.D.* and that reproductive rights for women remained a central concern for her beyond the 1890s. Her diaries and autobiography reveal her potential anxieties with artificial methods for reproductive intervention and control. Although her autobiography suggests her defense of artificial insemination, Meyer's sketch in her personal diary indicates a critique toward artificial birth control methods, particularly when overused. Meyer does categorize her unpublished novel as a satire, not unlike Gilman's *Herland*. It is unlikely, therefore, that Meyer truly believes women will lose their natural reproductive functions, or that the human race, generally, and male sex, specifically, risks extinction from lack of natural births. Instead, Meyer's sketch returns to a familiar theme in her writing, one she most fully articulated in *Helen Brent, M.D.*: Sex education.

After *Helen Brent, M.D.*, Meyer wrote what she considered her "major opus," *Robert Annys: Poor Priest* (1901), a historical novel about a fourteenth-century priest who seeks to educate his lower-class and poverty-stricken parishioners in spite of Roman Catholic ordinances that discourage education, especially reading, among peasants. Meyer later briefly abandoned novel-writing for playwriting. Although she would eventually despair of becoming a successful novelist or dramatist, she continued writing until her death, producing no less than 350 published letters to the editor, many short stories and plays, and three memoirs. She and her husband had one child, a daughter, Margaret, who was born in 1894 and died from an accidental, self-inflicted gunshot wound in 1923. Following her daughter's untimely death, Meyer became increasingly involved in political issues. She volunteered with the National Association for the Advancement of Colored People and worked with several NAACP leaders, including James Weldon Johnson, to raise funds for black college students. She also wrote several essays denouncing Nazi policy as anti-Semitic, and remained committed to the anti-suffrage movement even after Congress passed the nineteenth amendment.

The "Anti" Feminist Manifesto

Meyer was not always considered feminist among her contemporaries and scholars. Her feminist associations were tenuous, and remain so in academic discourse, because Meyer aligned herself with the anti-suffrage movement. In *It's Been Fun*, Meyer acknowledges this tension between her defense of women's rights and her critique of suffrage, remarking "[p]erhaps it seems odd that one who fought so hard for higher education for women should have been against giving them the vote" (202). She continues, offering "precise reasons" for her anti-suffrage sympathies: "Antis had always stood for conscientious use of the ballot, once it was ours," yet it should not be "ours" until women achieve a fair education (205). Meyer feared irresponsible and ignorant voting, a position many Antis held, explains Manuela

Thurner. Antis and suffragists were not necessarily oppositional to one another; rather they were working toward the same goals—women's rights—but in different ways. Suffrage would introduce political parties into feminist social reform and political activism, and Antis feared bipartisanism would distract women from their role in organizing and executing social reform measures (Thurner 42). Higher education for women was among those social reform issues that Antis advocated. Because Antis placed it foremost in their advocacies, and before suffrage, they were critiqued by their suffragette contemporaries and are often considered "anti-feminist" among present-day critics.

Joyce Antler, for instance, declares Meyer "[s]tridently antifeminist," as a result of her anti-suffrage ties, and concedes that Meyer only returned to a "mixed feminism" in the 1920s, after the nineteenth amendment's passing (i.e., when suffrage no longer "mattered") (71). Although she believes Meyer "seemed destined even more than [her sister] Maud ... to make her mark as a feminist," Antler observes a shift in Meyer's politics after her marriage to Dr. Alfred Meyer (64). She speculates that Meyer's change in feminist politics during the first decade of the twentieth century was reactionary and in direct retaliation against her sister, Maud Nathan, of whom Antler claims Annie was jealous because of Maud's leadership role in the suffragist movement (66). Meyer's feminism certainly appears "mixed" from a historical perspective that associates *only* suffrage with feminism, but such generalized claims as sibling rivalry appear too simple in defining Meyer's feminist politics. Lynn D. Gordon reminds her readers that Meyer wrote several texts that fit squarely within the "feminist camp," including her edited volume *Woman's Work in America* and *Helen Brent, M.D.* (510). The latter clarifies Meyer's feminist politics, since she does not address suffrage at all but presents a didactic narrative that defends higher education and sex education for women.

Helen Brent, M.D. narrates one woman's struggle for public acceptance as a doctor and as a lady among the New York City elite while she privately struggles with her choice in pursuing marriage or career. Meyer's basic plot emerges from an established tradition among medical fiction from the last thirty years of the nineteenth century, namely a focus on the marriage-or-career narrative. Since Elizabeth Blackwell became the first woman to receive a medical diploma in the United States, graduating from New York's Geneva Medical College in 1849, fiction writers increasingly reflected on the cultural implications of these developments (Wegener 596). Many portrayals of "the doctress" were not flattering but stereotypical, even condescending, as in the case of William Dean Howells's *Doctor Breen's Practice* (1881) or Henry James's *The Bostonians* (1886). Amidst these portrayals rose a serious debate in medical discourse, both fictional and non-fictional: Could a female physician perform medical duties equal with her male counterparts, given her delicate constitution? If so, did this "masculine" behavior prevent her from participating in traditional female social roles such as marriage or motherhood?

Meyer responds with a "yes" to the former question and a hard "no" to the latter as she seeks to prove in her novel that female physicians are not hysterical and can perform medical duties equal with men. Helen Brent does not "faint or go into hysterics," as her male counterparts expect, but displays the "required nerve, coolness, daring, skill, a steady hand and a delicate one" when performing a hysterectomy on Mrs. Root (9). Meyer takes great pains in further proving that professional women—doctresses included—can participate in urban society as cultured ladies, for

Helen Brent not only holds office hours and sees patients, but also attends the opera, plays cards at high tea, and makes an appearance at important events in New York City elite society such as high-profile weddings. Meyer does, however, appear ambivalent as to whether female physicians should marry and bear children. Earlier lady-doctor novels expressed concerns that the work of female physicians might distract from their duties as wives and mothers. Elizabeth Stuart Phelps's Dr. Zay in her novel of the same name (1882) warns her beau that, should they marry, he might eventually feel "neglected" or "wronged": "'You would think of those other men,'" Zay continues, "'whose wives were always punctual at dinner in long dresses, and could play to them evenings, and accept invitations, and always be on hand, like the kitten'" (164). Sarah Orne Jewett's Dr. Nan Prince from *A Country Doctor* (1884) offers a similar position in her assertion that domestic and professional life "cannot be taken together in a woman's life as in a man's," since her attentions would be divided in a way that a man's would not (142).

Meyer finds this marriage-or-career dilemma a double standard, and further asserts that the question itself should not exist. Helen Brent's beau, Harold Skidmore, calls off their engagement, since Helen will not resign her medical practice for marriage. Although Helen attempts to negotiate with Harold, asserting, "I am willing to confine myself purely to consultation work and to performing operations," Harold will not compromise (18). For Harold Skidmore, marriage is an all-or-nothing contract. His future wife must devote her life's work to him and his household, or not at all. Harold is not convinced that Helen "can combine [her professional work] with the arduous duties of a housewife," as she claims (18), and further finds Helen's desire to work "unnatural" behavior for a woman (18–19). In reflecting upon her decision, Helen determines she does not regret choosing her career over marriage and, in fact, claims that such a decision should not be forced upon professional women at all. Men, she claims, "must be educated to allow greater liberty of thought and action to their wives" or else society will not progress and marriage as an institution will suffer (31).

At the close of the novel, Meyer leaves Helen's relationship with Harold open for possible reconciliation, since Harold is now a widower and has experienced personal growth from his marital trauma. Harold achieves his perfect marriage with a seemingly devoted and domestic wife, Louise Skidmore, but she is only playing a role. Marital duties suffocate Louise, as Helen predicts, and her affair with New York City's most-eligible bachelor, Mortimer Stuart Verplank, results in her syphilis-induced death. Harold, it is suggested, awakens to the realization that late nineteenth-century society enforces multiple double standards. On the one hand, women are discouraged from professional work while men are not; yet, men gain satisfaction from their professional work while women fall into depression from lack of professional work and their domestic duties. On the other hand, men are permitted, even expected, to seek extramarital sexual pleasures when they are unhappy in their domestic lives, while women are chastised for extramarital sexual activities even though they, too, often seek such pleasures as a means of escape from their unhappy domestic lives. Meyer does not condone sexual promiscuity among men or women, nor does she wholly blame the male sex for women's disenfranchisement. Dr. Brent warns her protégé, Lotus Bayley, that she "'must not make the mistake which many women make and cry out blindly against men,'" for "'women fail to understand us much more than men do'" (60). Meyer does, however, expose several double standards accepted by late nineteenth-century society, among them gendered social roles, marital expectations, and sexual behaviors.

Unlike earlier works of medical fiction, Meyer's *Helen Brent, M.D.* adopts a "self-consciously political" position concerned with sex education rather than simply offering a marriage-or-career narrative that defends a woman's right to professional work. Kristin Swenson identifies the emergence of the New Woman as initiating this shift in medical fiction. During the 1880s and 1890s, the New Woman became a feminist ideal referring to American women who rejected social conventions in favor of increased independence and autonomy.[7] The New Woman eschewed her "feminine" private sphere and the domestic roles therein for a "masculine" public sphere and professional work. She often married later or not at all, gained a college education, and developed her career in medicine, law, politics, or business. The New Woman was not always political, though suffragettes were considered a type of New Woman. Politics, however, is precisely what Swenson finds differentiates the New Woman doctor novel from earlier lady-doctor novels. Female physicians in lady-doctor

---

[7] Henry James coined the term "New Woman" in reference to "American women of affluence and sensitivity" who were predominately "[y]oung and unmarried" and "rejected social conventions, especially those imposed on women." James warns women against developing such radical sentiments and speaks of them in a derogatory manner. Many women, however, embraced the term and considered New Womanhood a positive attribute rather than a negative one. By the early twentieth century, the term came to embody far more women than simply those in middle- to upper-class society with "affluence and sensitivity." (Smith-Rosenberg 176)

novels, Swenson claims, such as Phelps's *Dr. Zay* and Jewett's *A Country Doctor*, do not challenge established medical practices, but participate within the (patriarchal) system. Female physicians in the New Woman doctor novel, on the other hand, challenge current medical practices and the ideologies underpinning such practices that relegate women within established gender roles based on their biological sex.

Swenson specifically identifies Annie Nathan Meyer's *Helen Brent, M.D.* as perhaps *the* quintessential New Woman doctor novel, and Helen Brent as a model New Woman. Although *Helen Brent, M.D.* is not the first New Woman doctor novel, it is the first work of medical fiction to represent a female allopathic physician, and a gynecologist, moreover. In choosing allopathic medicine rather than homeopathic medicine, Meyer initiates a radical—and political—shift in the genre of medical fiction. Her narrative technique suggests women not only can perform established gynecological practices such as sexual surgeries but are also authorities in medical discourse. In making her protagonist and titular character a New Woman, Meyer also raises questions regarding medical ethics in gynecological practice and scientific knowledge construction, specifically gendered diseases and limited sex education.

In several places throughout the novel, Helen Brent laments the negative implications that urban elite social behavior imposes on women's health, but none are as dire as the threat of venereal disease, which appears rampant among New York City's elite in Meyer's novel. Like her fictional contemporaries, including Alcott's Dr. Alex Campbell in *Eight Cousins* (1874) or Gilman's Dr. Jane Bellair in *The Crux* (1911), Dr. Helen Brent acknowledges such conditions as pneumonia "result from inadequate clothing of the

fashionable evening world" and hysteria is caused by "the constant
strain that social duties lay upon the entire nervous system" (34).
In such moments, Meyer winks toward popular political and social
reform issues including dress reform and marriage rights, which
reveals her awareness of the social pressures negatively impacting
women's health, reproductive or otherwise. However, Meyer tackles
social purity reform in the plot of *Helen Brent, M.D.* and insists
current medical practices, not women's bodies, are responsible for
its perpetuation.

Dr. Brent first discoverers Mortimer Stuart Verplank suffers
from syphilis when her unnamed patient, a girl with "fair skin"
and "pretty, soft, blonde hair that told of former beauty" visits her
during office hours (40). The patient is homeless and no hospital
will admit her "because [her] baby didn't live," but was stillborn
(40). The patient herself is doomed either to death or a fate
worse than death as a diseased woman "whose physical condition
was utterly ruined" (41). She might have been of the elite class
before her fall from grace through extramarital relations with
Mr. Verplank, or she might have been a prostitute. Nonetheless,
Dr. Brent admits the patient, using her interaction with the
patient as a teaching moment for Meyer's audience. Throughout
the nineteenth century, "venereal disease" and "prostitute"
became nearly synonymous (Spongberg 10), and Meyer's readers
would therefore likely consider Dr. Brent's patient as deserving
of her fate. Because nineteenth-century medical practitioners
pathologized women's bodies, and especially the body of the
prostitute, nineteenth-century readers would likely find Dr. Brent's
patient solely responsible for the death of her newborn.

It is significant, then, that Dr. Brent does not blame her
patient or Mr. Verplank, but instead blames nineteenth-century

gynecological practices and its "conspiracy of silence." Having discovered Mortimer Stuart Verplank as responsible for her patient's illness and impending death, Helen Brent visits the mother of his betrothed, Rose Bayley. Mrs. Bayley expresses little concern with her future son-in-law's health, nor does she recognize the "double standard" extant in New York society: "Now, my dear doctor, you don't really think that I have thought a handsome young fellow with such an enormous fortune could very well have lived the life of a saint?" (43). Mrs. Bayley's response represents nineteenth-century readers' own cultural assumptions, since as Mary Spongberg claims, any nineteenth-century reader would recognize that middle- and upper-class men "had an investment both in maintaining the notion of female purity and an investment in violating it" (10). Men could relieve their sexual urges and still make prudent marriages, yet women were not privy to such social—or sexual—behaviors; rather, they must remain chaste inside and outside marriage.

Medical practitioners upheld these social norms simply by withholding information from their patients, a practice Allan Brandt refers to as the "conspiracy of silence" (23–24). In other words, medical practitioners did not educate their patients, either male or female, on such basic health conditions as puberty, sexual intercourse, or venereal disease contraction, since these subjects were "too delicate," especially for women. Thus, in consummating their marriages, women were often surprised to find their husbands not only experienced in sexual intercourse, but also already suffering symptoms of syphilis or gonorrhea. Rose Bayley not only produces a stillborn child just as did her husband's lover but also dies from syphilis, having never known what caused her illness or newborn's death. Dr. Brent and Mrs. Bayley, however, do recognize the cause of Rose's death, and both feel responsible for not apprising Rose of her husband's health condition. Although she had warned Mrs. Bayley that Rose's marriage would literally kill her, "[w]hen Helen stood over Rose's body she felt like a murderer" nonetheless (48). Mrs. Bayley expresses similar guilt, "for now the completely broken woman" "hysterically reiterated that she had killed her only child, her only child" (48).

It is precisely in moments such as these—Rose Bayley's death and funeral—that Meyer reminds readers what is at stake in sex education: It is a matter of life and death. Dr. Brent reminds Mrs. Bayley that she has another daughter, Lotus, for whom she is responsible. She must not make the same mistakes that she made with Rose, Dr. Brent insists, but to no avail. Helen Brent takes it upon herself to properly educate Lotus Bayley, social hygiene and all. As Dr. Brent explains to Lotus her purpose for becoming a doctor, "[m]y chief aim in working" as a gynecologist "is to make women find themselves … in every sense of the word, [find] themselves; [find] their complete, rounded selves" (62). One aspect of a woman's self-identity involves her sexual hygiene, a point Meyer makes repeatedly in the deaths of Helen Brent's three patients—her unnamed hospital patient, Rose Bayley, and Louise Skidmore—all of whom die from contracting syphilis. Although the culprit is Mortimer Stuart Verplank, Dr. Brent does not blame him but those medical practices underpinning social behavior. She chastises women for perpetuating the "conspiracy of silence" as much, if not more, than she chastises men, as in the case of Mrs. Keith-Brew, who knew of Louise's affair with Mortimer and said nothing.

Sex and the City—and Syphilis

Between 1874 and 1916, several women writers would adopt "self-consciously political" positions toward women's reproductive health in works of medical fiction, among them Rebecca Harding Davis, Louisa May Alcott, and Charlotte Perkins Gilman. These women wrote during a period in which language was censored, since then-postmaster general Anthony Comstock passed a national law prohibiting the production and distribution of "obscene" literature. This federal act, passed on March 3, 1873, was officially titled the Act for the Suppression of Trade in, and Circulation of, Obscene Literature and Articles of Immoral Use. Although the law primarily referred to contraception and abortion, it also banned written material—including books—that contained information on "any indecent or immoral purpose." Such vague rhetoric allowed for broad interpretation, and sex education often fell under "indecent" and "immoral" purposes. Novel-reading also received a reputation for indecency and immorality, since in the nineteenth century, fiction often served political purposes. Instead of simply offering "aesthetic pleasure," many fictional works provided an imaginative stimulus for writers and readers alike in their shared attempts at proposing solutions for social ills (Tompkins xi).

This is not to say that non-fictional texts were apolitical or that they did not address reproductive health. Many prominent feminists and social reformers addressed reproductive health in their essays and advice manuals. Julia Ward Howe, Eliza Duffey, and Anna Brackett famously responded to Dr. Edward H. Clarke's *Sex and Education: A Fair Chance for the Girls* in their own advice manuals defending sex education. Lavinia Dock and Emma Goldman both wrote essays for the social purity movement, and, like Annie Nathan Meyer, they argued that venereal diseases did not originate in women. Margaret Sanger edited and wrote for the *Birth Control Review*, and produced no less than five books and several pamphlets in defense of birth control. Fiction, however, performs a kind of cultural work specific to its genre in that it does not simply present a didactic argument or offer solutions for reform. Because fiction mirrors reality but is not itself factual, fiction holds the potential for "remaking the social and political order" by inciting the reader's imagination with alternative ways in which real-life events might unfold (Tompkins xvii). Physicians and their patients might engage in more candid conversations, Meyer suggests. The Mrs. Bayleys of the world might educate their daughters about what to expect in the marriage bed, and if they themselves are not aware of such health risks, mothers might provide better resources for their daughters such as advice manuals or consultations with a female physician.

The scenarios Annie Nathan Meyer presents in *Helen Brent, M.D.*, many of which may have been familiar to her readers, offer a blueprint for how to act in such situations so as to resist the "conspiracy of silence" engendered by nineteenth-century medical practitioners and Comstockian censorship. Yet, these same scenarios also reveal reproductive health as a primary concern for early feminists, one that has been overlooked in our historical narrative of the early women's rights movement. *Helen Brent, M.D.* is culturally significant, and in need of recovery, precisely for this reason: It offers previously unrecognized findings on early feminism and the field of gynecology during the *fin de siècle*. Reproductive rights and sex education are, perhaps, not wholly twentieth- or twenty-first-century phenomena; rather, their roots stretch back to the late nineteenth century. Annie Nathan Meyer is not the only writer whose work reveals such intimate associations between feminism and medical science, or nineteenth-century feminists and contemporary feminists. She does, however, provide an authentic voice that emerges from the birthplace of gynecology itself, New York City.

Acknowledgments

I wish to thank the American Jewish Archives for granting permission to conduct archival research on this project. I am particularly grateful for Kevin Proffitt's careful attention to my research needs at the archive, and to Gail Madden for arranging my stay on campus in the Sisterhood Dormitory at Hebrew Union College. Finally, I wish to thank the College of Liberal Arts at the University of Texas at Dallas for funding my research travel to the American Jewish Archives in Cincinnati, Ohio.

Works Cited

Antler, Joyce. *The Journey Home: How Jewish Women Shaped Modern America.* New York: Pantheon Books, 1997.

Barker-Benfield, Ben. "Sexual Surgery in Late Nineteenth Century America." *International Journal of Health Services* 5, 2 (1975): 279–98.

Brandt, Allan M. *No Magic Bullet: A Social History of Venereal Disease in the United States Since 1880.* New York: Oxford University Press, 1985.

Browner, Stephanie P. *Profound Science and Elegant Literature Imagining Doctors in Nineteenth-Century America.* Philadelphia: University of Pennsylvania Press, Inc., 2011.

Carey, Jane. "The Racial Imperatives of Sex: Birth Control and
    Eugenics in Britain, the United States, and Australia in
    the Interwar Years." *Women's History Review* 21, 5 (2012):
    733–52.

Gilder, Jeanette. Letter to Annie Nathan Meyer. 29 March 1892.
    MS numbered album 7, Annie Nathan Meyer Papers
    Collection, Box 1, Folder 1. The Jacob Rader Marcus Center
    of the American Jewish Archives, Hebrew Union College.

Goldenberg, Myrna Gallant. "Annie Nathan Meyer: Barnard
    Godmother and Gotham Gadfly." Dissertation, University of
    Maryland—College Park, 1987.

Gordon, Lynn D. "Annie Nathan Meyer and Barnard College:
    Mission and Identity in Women's Higher Education, 1889–
    1950." *History of Education Quarterly* 26, 4 (1986): 503–22.

Haller, John S. and Robin M. Haller. *The Physician and Sexuality in
    Victorian America.* New York: W. W. Norton and Company,
    Inc., 1974.

McGregor, Deborah Kuhn. *From Midwives to Medicine: The
    Birth of American Gynecology.* New Brunswick, NJ: Rutgers
    University Press, 1998.

Meyer, Annie Nathan. Diary. MS numbered album 7, Annie
    Nathan Meyer Papers Collection, Box 12, Folder 5. The
    Jacob Rader Marcus Center of the American Jewish Archives,
    Hebrew Union College.

———. *Helen Brent, M.D.* (1892). Hastings, NE: Hastings College
    Press, 2018.

———. *It's Been Fun: An Autobiography.* New York: Schuman,
    1966.

Rhodes, Chip. "Social Protest, Reform, and the American Political
    Novel." *A Companion to the American Novel,* First Edition.

Ed. Alfred Bendixen. Oxford: Blackwell Publishing Ltd.,
2012. 187–205.

Smith-Rosenberg, Carroll. *Disorderly Conduct: Visions of Gender in
Victorian America*. Oxford: Oxford University Press, 1985.

Spongberg, Mary. *Feminizing Venereal Disease: The Body of the
Prostitute in Nineteenth-Century Medical Discourse*. New York:
New York University Press, 1997.

Swenson, Kristin. *Medical Women and Victorian Fiction*. Columbia:
University of Missouri Press, 2005.

Thurner, Manuela. "'Better Citizens Without the Ballot': American
Anti-Suffrage Women and Their Rational During the
Progressive Era." *Journal of Women's History* 5, 1 (1993):
33–60.

Tompkins, Jane. *Sensational Designs: The Cultural Work of American
Fiction, 1790–1860*. New York: Oxford University Press,
1985.

Wegener, Frederick. "The Literary Representation of Women
Doctors in the United States, 1860–1920." *Literature
Compass* 4, 3 (2007): 576–98.

....

Dr. Stephanie Peebles Tavera is Assistant Professor of English at Texas A&M University–Central Texas. She is the author of a forthcoming book with Edinburgh University Press on women's medical fiction written during a period of censorship under Comstock Law, which is tentatively titled "Un(dis)covered Bodies: Science, Narrative, and the Female Body in Feminist Medical Fiction." Her fields of expertise include American women's literature, medical humanities, and feminist disability studies.

Helen Brent, M.D.

I

One bright, warm spring afternoon, there was a large and
enthusiastic crowd assembled in West —th Street. The occasion
was the laying of the corner stone of the Root Memorial Hospital
and College for Women. The crowd was enormous. All the seats
were filled, many people were standing far out into the roadway,
and at all the available windows were eager faces; even upon some
of the neighboring roofs there were spectators looking down upon
the sight. It was a fashionable crowd, for the Root Memorial
had been the topic of the town for the past two years. This is its
peculiar history:

For some time it had been rumored about that the wealthy
Mrs. Root had determined to give a large sum to some worthy
object in memory of her greatly lamented spouse, Phineas Root.
Poor Mrs. Root (and I say that advisedly, although her personal
fortune was estimated at something between twenty-five and thirty
millions) had no sooner allowed this whisper to get abroad than
she was subjected to the most fearful martyrdom. There was not a
college professor throughout the country that did not see himself
the honored head of a department that "never before had been
able to offer such unique opportunities for research through the
munificent gift of Mrs. Root"; there was not a babies' hospital,
not a society for the distribution of tracts among the heathen,
not an association for the suppression of vice, not a sewing circle
that did not bring forward its just and peculiar claims in the most
eloquent terms. The world soon found out which church could

boast the honor of being guardian to the soul and thirty millions of the renowned Mrs. Root, and there was not a church of that denomination (I am not going to commit myself) from Texas to Maine that did not assume the right to "Propagate the divine gospel as it never could have been done before," "To sweep sin from the face of the earth," and all by means of Mrs. Root's millions.

A sharp struggle waged at home between the minister and the physician, that together bore the responsibility of caring for Mrs. Root's physical and spiritual welfare. The Reverend Dr. Harkless argued that nothing would assure the everlasting peace of the late lamented so completely as the erection of a magnificent church with expressly imported bronze doors, stained glass windows, organ, carved pews, etc., and last, but not least, a snugly fitted-up parsonage. But the wily Dr. Snowborough, on the other hand, insisted that nothing would comfort the dear departed so much as the knowledge that a deserved tribute had been paid to "that honorable profession [striking his breast], that honorable and self-sacrificing body of men through whose efforts he had been allowed to enjoy the good things of life years after it was thought impossible by the members of the clergy—meaning no disrespect to that honored body, of course."

It was true that plain, homely, life-loving Phineas had never shown any particular fondness for his pale, cadaverous clergyman; while he had been devoted to his rubicund doctor, who had possessed the decided advantage of being able to sit down to a quiet "rubber" now and then. So Dr. Snowborough had the best of the argument until one day a letter arrived from a far-away town in the depths of Colorado suggesting that Devil's Gulch was the proper place to be the recipient of Mrs. Root's "munificent gift." Devil's Gulch, so the letter stated, was the place where the late Phineas had first struck gold, and what could be more fitting, than that a palatial art museum be erected there? The mayor of Devil's Gulch was convinced that the presence of such an art museum would do much towards doing away with the erection of gambling dens—he regretted the undue proportion of them at present—and he ended with a magnificent peroration upon the means of securing such a museum. He knew through excellent authority that the Italian government was quite ready to give up the art treasures of the Vatican and the Pitti Palace to American enterprise (if backed by the necessary cash), and he would stake his professional reputation upon the success and glory attached to such an unprecedented achievement. Besides, the glory of Colorado would thus be assured. The late Phineas Root was an American, and he was proud of it! To give a memorial to the effete civilization of the East is to knuckle down basely before the prejudices of the European aristocracy. The West, the wild, the free, the glorious West, is the only real America, etc., etc.

Now, to the thorough-going New Yorker there is a potent and mysterious charm in giving money far away; it would be inexplicable otherwise that so many of the great magnates of the metropolis love to put up all sorts of memorials throughout the length and breadth of the land—in Nevada, Colorado, Tennessee, Maine, anywhere, but in the city which ought to claim, at least a portion, of their allegiance. Perhaps it is because New York attracts to itself all the wealth of this vast country and each millionaire keeps in his heart a soft corner for his native home. He that gained his wealth through the richness of California's soil, is not apt to forget his debt; he that owes it to the coals of Pennsylvania, gives generously to that anthracite quarter; and he that has cause to bless the hams of Cincinnati, or the beef of Chicago, forgets not to show his thankfulness. Although his body is comfortably ensconced in New York, his heart is never there for a moment.

There was a peculiar fascination about the argument used by the mayor of Devil's Gulch. Let us not go too deeply into the why and the wherefore, suffice it to say that the two doctors began to scent a powerful rival in the field, and their efforts were renewed with even more than their former enthusiasm. It was agreed between them that they should permit the erection of two memorials, anything rather than let the coveted gift slip altogether out of their grasp.

Meanwhile, Mrs. Root fell ill with a trouble that seemed to baffle the greatest efforts of her physician. The days went by and it looked as if the great memorial would have to include one for herself as well. But Mrs. Root did not hanker after that distinction, and she listened eagerly when a friend assured her that there was only one way of being cured and that was by changing her physician and taking Dr. Brent, a woman doctor. Of this particular Dr. Brent the friend related the most wonderful tales of marvelous cures: there was Mrs. A., who had not walked for years until Dr. Brent took her in hand; Mrs. C, who had been utterly miserable until Dr. Brent performed a most dangerous operation upon her. In short, Mrs. Root's ears were filled with so many stories of the fame and success of Dr. Brent, that, conservative as she was, and not quite sure that she approved of "those women doctors," she followed in the footsteps of the fashion, and the new doctor was appealed to.

The story goes on to tell that Dr. Brent successfully performed an operation on Mrs. Root, who from that time became the doctor's most devoted slave—hence the final outcome of the much discussed "Root Memorial." For once rumor was to be trusted. Dr. Brent had really performed an exceedingly difficult and dangerous operation, and although it was not two years since her return from Europe, where she had been studying, it was true that she was justly celebrated for the treatment of her own sex. It is needless to say that the fame of Dr. Brent was immeasurably increased by the fact that she had successfully operated upon a woman with thirty millions—the presence of so many millions requiring extraordinary skill, of course. Divine power of wealth! Far-reaching, embracing into its magic circle myriads of lesser mortals, glorified by the remotest contact with it! Poor, plain, little Miss Perkins is taken up enthusiastically because she teaches the alphabet to the red-haired, diminutive descendants of the glorious Phineas; Miss Cuticle is the rage because it is discovered that to her falls the difficult task of being manicure to thirty millions (rather confusing rhetoric, but justified by usage in the *Daily Sensation,* the *Weekly Shocks,* and other standard journals of the day); the milliner and dressmaker of Mrs. Root are sure to share the effulgent halo, not-withstanding the execrable taste of their celebrated customer. Then there was the talented young Brush, who never had succeeded in selling a picture until his "Love in a Cottage" had been discovered hanging upon the "sumptuous walls of Mrs. Root's palatial mansion"; and there was Brick, the architect, who has made his fortune since he designed the garden-house that "graces the magnificent lawn of Mrs. Root's dreamlike palace at Newport." Again, say I, "Oh, glorious power of wealth, all hail!"

To go back to the laying of the corner-stone, as I have said before, the crowd was a very fashionable one. Dr. Brent's feat was no ordinary triumph; there was not only the triumph of wresting the memorial from the hands of those Devil's Gulch people, and of actually persuading a New Yorker to let her money remain

within the city limits; but there was the additional triumph on top
of that of securing a gift from a woman in the cause of women.
Especially in the line of education; it had so long been the tradition
of wealthy women to swell the coffers of educational institutions at
which the just rights of their own sex had been persistently ignored,
that this action of Mrs. Root in founding a woman's college
electrified the city.

Then there was also the superb triumph of having the great
Dr. Thaddeus Manning address the meeting, to be seen publicly
championing the cause of woman's progress. Dr. Manning had
done his very best to shut out women from the advantages of the
Fudge Hospital for Women, of whose medical board he was the
honored president. Some years before Dr. Brent had refused to
be conquered; and had made her way in as a modest interne. It
seems that the persevering Dr. Brent had raked up a pretty bit of
scandal and there threatened to arise a good deal of talk. She had
discovered that the hospital owed its endowment to an eccentric
old lady, who twenty years before had had enough faith in her
sex to found the hospital in the interests of women, for their
treatment, and for their clinical instruction. Trusting Miss Fudge
had departed this earth before the building was completed, and
had reposed perfect confidence in old Dr. Manning, the father of
the present doctor, who for some reason totally ignored the wishes
of the departed Miss Fudge, and no woman medical student or
physician had ever been permitted to enter the sacred precincts.
But now Dr. Thaddeus Manning could no longer stand up against
current opinion, and he was clever enough to give way in time to
save himself from ungallant defeat. Lately the shrewd doctor (who
could measure the pulse of the times as well as of his patients) had
put himself upon the top crest of popularity by inviting Dr. Brent

to meet him in consultation over the case of a well-known society lady.

The trustees of the Fudge Hospital for Women had become very much agitated when the rumor was circulated that Dr. Brent had secured the magnificent Root Memorial to endow a great hospital and college for women. The board of trustees, backed by the medical board, reconsidered its past policy and unanimously elected Dr. Brent attending physician. But it was too late: Dr. Brent was not to be caught so easily as that. She was shrewd enough to see that Dr. Brent, comparatively unknown and wanting to serve as interne, was quite a different being from Dr. Brent, well known, popular, and bearing in her hands the Root millions.

The great event of the day was the new president's address, the president of the Root Memorial. As she stood there bowing before the enthusiastic audience (she could see the exquisitely gloved hands of Dr. Manning clapping approval), she was a woman to bring a glow of enthusiasm to anyone's heart. To look at her you would never suspect she was guilty of having graduated from a co-educational college, of having served as the only woman interne in the Fudge Hospital, of having gone to Germany alone and braved the medical lions in their dens, of having been the one woman that the great and only Professor Schwetterberger had consented to instruct, and of having performed, on her return to America, difficult gynecological operations, the success of which had interested the entire medical profession—operations that required nerve, coolness, daring, skill, a steady hand and a delicate one; and when they were over she had never been known either to faint or go into hysterics, as in the past Dr. Manning had prophesied would be the conduct of the woman physician.

As she stood there, she looked like a very handsome, amiable woman, surely not past thirty, and very tastefully and quietly dressed. Her fine figure and beautiful face made her a walking commentary on the usual opinion that "Mind is an enemy to beauty." Thin, sallow, overworked school ma'ams, and big, striding women reporters, who themselves failed obviously to maintain the proper mental and physical equilibrium, always pointed to Dr. Brent as a refutation of a theory that they might be presumed to prove. One of the evening papers gave the following description (and by the way, before I quote it, I wonder why it is that newspaper reporters always go into the details of a woman's dress, whether at a suffrage caucus or a prayer meeting? Just fancy the papers containing an account of a costume worn by the Hon. Grover Cleveland when he delivers an address on some auspicious occasion. Fancy having the mind distracted by the color of his necktie or the check of his trousers. And yet, let his wife show herself for a moment and her dress is pounced upon, every detail is seized and we are regaled the following day by a wonderful description of the—upon each occasion—handsomest and most tasteful costume she has yet worn. I beg their pardon; they would not descend to such vulgar English. I should have said "that had yet adorned the lovely figure").

The extract from the *Evening Whirl* reads thus, and, allowing for a certain amount of reportorial hyperbole, it is a pretty fair account:

The scene beggars description; the metropolis' fairest dames and haughtiest seigneurs were on hand. The Four Hundred, led by its genial leader, was there. Who was not there? Surely no one would care to confess one's absence.... A strange sight was witnessed by the representative of the *Evening Whirl*. A man worth $100,000,000 stood unconsciously gazing at the sight, shoulder to shoulder with an Irish hod-carrier. Two things were especially notable: the hod-carrier did not look at all abashed, and the fact that the man who could sign a check for $100,000,000 should be obliged to stand up.

The report goes on to say:

Of course our lady readers will want to know all about the successful winner of the Root Memorial Prize.... Dr. Brent stood confidently upon the platform, perfectly at her ease. She is superbly tall, and the figure of a very Juno. The expression of her face is peculiarly soft and winning; yet the high forehead, unmarred by either bang or curl, and the rather square jaw, betoken the presence of will and determination. Her orbs are of a lustrous, deep sapphire, and her hair, which was simply caught up in a loose coil, and fastened with a large tortoise-shell pin, is of a rare golden chestnut shade. Many were surprised who now, for the first time, were looking upon the renowned pupil of Professor Schwetterberger.... To complete the picture, I will add that Dr. Brent was clad in a garment of some sort of soft, clinging material of sapphire blue, just the color to bring out her deep eyes (but then we do not dare accuse the learned doctor of possessing any of the weaknesses of her sex); while upon the golden chestnut crest reposed a dainty little bonnet of dark-blue straw, and we will add that its strings were neatly tied, and not hanging in a slovenly stream down her back, as, doubtless, some of those present expected to see them.

The address of the new president was a masterly one, and no one was disappointed, not even her warmest admirers. She began with an account of the position of women in medicine half a century ago, and gave a concise, but wonderfully interesting sketch of their heroic efforts to obtain recognition. The time was past when women had to struggle for the legal right to practice, or for recognition from the medical organizations; but the present problem was to enable women to obtain the best possible training for the profession. She drew a vivid picture of the early struggles of the pioneer women doctors to pick up the necessary knowledge in stray crumbs, eagerly going hither and thither, thankful for whatever little was thrown to them. She led up to the present day, when women have received so much that nothing but the very best ought to have any significance. The day of crumb picking has gone. The need of to-day is the very best training, equal to that received by the profession. But the new college would not be content with following the institutions at which men received their training. It would not be a mere repetition; it was going to open out a new field of work to American physicians; it would hold up the very highest scientific standards, and it was hoped that the men would follow in their track.

She ended with these words, spoken from her very soul:

"And yet it has been proved, I think, that woman, in assuming these new duties and responsibilities, need not cast aside any of the great responsibilities which she has inherited from the past ages. The new womanhood is a development, an enriching of the old womanhood—not, in any sense, a narrowing down, nor a dwarfing of our noblest conceptions. It means growth in every direction."

As she uttered those words, evidently struggling to suppress emotion, her eyes met the glance of a young man who stood in the crowd leaning up against a lamppost, and who had been watching her earnestly. Dr. Brent's eyes fell to the ground, and some say they saw tears in them.

The applause burst forth rapturously, there was even some faint suggestion of cheering, so deeply had her speech awakened interest and sympathy. The man who stood watching her shut his eyes in pain when the loud applause broke out, and shrugged his shoulders angrily. However, he was the first one to reach the platform and congratulate her. He looked straight into her face, as he said, in a low voice:

"Helen, I wish I could honestly wish you happiness in your new career."

Helen flushed and then turned pale, so pale that someone offered her a chair, saying, "I am afraid you have overestimated your strength." And the young man repeated, but with a new significance:

"Yes, I fear Dr. Brent has overestimated her strength," and lifting his hat politely, he was soon making his way through the throng of people that gathered to offer congratulations.

II

When Helen had returned from Europe, Harold Skidmore had been one of the first to call upon her. Although he had broken their engagement when she had taken her doctor's degree, he yet hoped to conquer and to regain his old influence over her. Their affection for each other had begun way back when they were school children together, and he had been very miserable while she was abroad and had resolved to do whatever he could to bring her to reason. He was not at fault; he had only done what any man would have done.

She greeted him very calmly and they had discussed the usual conventional nothings that are the refuge of embarrassed people. At last, upon looking about the cosy study, and seeing her seated there so happily, so much as if she belonged there, and meant to remain there, Harold reached forth blindly, helplessly, across the chasm which he felt was cruelly widening as time went on. He was irritated at seeing her so beautiful and so strong. He had expected, now it was clear to him that he had hoped, that she would return worn out, tired of struggling, vexed by the cold hostilities of the German professors, and ready to fall into his protecting arms, for rest and peace. And what a rude tumble for his dream! He was sensible enough to see that there was no sympathy, no protection needed here. That smiling, calm woman sitting opposite him had the appearance of having walked all her life through a path of smiles and roses. He was conscious of a bit of humor in the situation. Where had fled all his masculine sense of superior power?

15

"So," he exclaimed, suddenly, looking about the room. "So you are here, really launched forth on your career?" He could not resist adding, "are you happy?"

"Very," quietly answered Helen.

"And so you really intend to settle down here a determined old maid, and have no greater outlook into the future than pursuing your profession and living here all alone?"

"Is it worth while to revive all this painful discussion?" she asked.

"Painful?" Harold repeated, pettishly. "I never thought it was painful to you."

"Then you are very unjust."

"No, a woman that can deliberately give up a man's love, a wife's sphere, the only true and real life for a woman, is not capable of suffering. If you really loved me, you would have given up all this, your ambition, your profession—everything. That is love."

"Is it?"

"Is it? How can you ask such a question? That only goes to prove—"

"I repeat, is it a man's love? I am aware that it is a man's idea of what a woman's love ought to be—for him. But it is very different from his conception of what his own love ought to be."

"Pshaw!"

"What man is capable of giving up all his ideals—the life for which he knows himself best fitted—of giving up his ambition, everything that makes life worth struggling for, that lifts it from mere animal existence, to give this all up for his love? To begin with, it is never demanded, so you men are never honestly put to the test. But once tried, I do not believe I know one man that would relinquish all this—what you now blandly wave aside as 'everything' for the love of any woman, to attain the sphere of a husband, a father, the only true and real life for any noble man."

"Helen, how you go on! The idea of comparing the ambition of a man, his very career, his breadwinning, with the day dreams of a woman."

"There you are. A man looks upon his own aims as justifiable, serious. Nothing must come in their way to thwart them. But a woman! She can have no aims; they are but idle whims, dreams, hobbies—what you will. It seems to me so futile to discuss it all over now after all these years. It was clear to me when you broke our engagement five years ago that we were utterly unsympathetic, and that is the end of it. Any man that considers a woman's life as less real, less earnest, less important, in every way than his own, can never be the man I could marry. You know I am no actress, Harold; you know I have never pretended to have forgot or grown out of my love for you. I have been always ready to say: 'I love you.' You will never appreciate what my decision cost me, but I cannot, I have no right to put aside my whole life, to sink my entire past and future into oblivion to suit your prejudices, for they amount to nothing more nor less."

"But let us seriously discuss it, Helen: haven't you really put it out of my power to marry you? How could you possibly attend to household duties; how could you call your time your own, much less mine; how much of yourself could you give up to home life, without giving up your practice?"

"I have before answered all this. I think marriage means the yielding of a great deal from both man and woman. Again I repeat that I would give up a great deal. I am prepared to make certain sacrifices, as a wife. On the contrary, you, as a husband, are ready to make none, cannot even see that there could possibly be any occasion to make any on your part. Is it not so? I have said I am willing to confine myself purely to consultation work and to performing operations. A consulting surgeon has great command over the disposal of her time."

Harold shuddered to think of his wife coming to him fresh from performing an operation, smelling of ether and carbolic acid.

"I shall name my own appointments, and while you are busy down town you will probably never see nor hear anything directly of them. I am confident I can combine this with the arduous duties of a housewife, even if I accept the clinic at the hospital. You know I am very strong. I don't promise you, mind you, to descend into the kitchen and bake the bread myself, but I do promise you that you'll get it of a fine and digestible quality."

Harold smiled. "This would be Elysium, but I wish I could believe you. I confess it scents of fairyland to me to hear you honestly say that you could be a doctor and not neglect things at home."

Helen rose. "I warned you that there was not the slightest use of our going over the ground again. Let us agree never to bring this up again, otherwise I cannot consent to see you. I cannot go over and over it; it is to no purpose."

Harold rose also, but remained sullenly silent.

"Can you not see," she continued, "how impossible it is that we shall ever agree? I shall shock you very much, I am afraid, but I may as well tell you I think you have just as much right to ask me to give up my profession as I have to ask you to give up yours."

This did surprise Harold, who slowly sat down again.

"What! you really think that? You go to ridiculous extremes."

"Why not? Have we not both devoted our lives, our hopes, and thoughts to our professions? Are we not both remorselessly ambitious, or to put it in another way, are we not both determined to leave the world better than we found it; are we not both convinced that not only we need our profession, but that our profession needs us? And suppose I said to you, 'I am afraid to marry you; surely you will neglect me; the stress of your profession must necessarily take you a great deal away. I don't want to have to sit at home while you are busy down town, detained by an important case; I do not wish to be left behind when you are obliged to take flying trips to Washington and Albany; I dare not link my life to yours unless you will give up your law, unless you go into some humdrum business that will permit you to devote yourself to your wife.' What would you think of me? How would you answer me? And yet I think your wife would be compelled to make as many sacrifices as my husband would. Where is the difference, only that I have faith, and you have not?"

"Absurd! preposterous! is it not the man that is the natural breadwinner?"

"Ah! so even you fall back on that old argument. How delightfully American! Moneymaking, then, is to be the *summun bonum* of life. The value of an individual lies in the amount of money he or she can make? Then you would require a man that writes the most exquisite poetry to give up the pen and rock the cradle, for his wife can probably make more by taking in washing."

Harold put out his hand deprecatingly. "How you run on," he said. "However, I cannot attempt to change the world. It is generally conceded that a man's career is more important than his wife's. It is so in the nature of things."

Helen made answer, "Then I shall never marry until I can find the man that together with me will be courageous enough to try to change the world." She held out her hand, "Good-by."

Harold took her hand. "You are entering upon a futile search."

Helen smiled.

"I did not mean to leave you with the impression that it was to be my sphere in life, to carry on such a search." She might have made a different answer. She might have said she had found that man in Germany (of all countries!) but her love for Harold had been too strong. It would have been a life of peace, of sympathy— there was respect, a good deal of affection. It was a temptation, but she knew her heart beat at the thought, the sight, the touch of another man.

III

After this conversation Harold had left Helen in anger; he had left her feeling as if all love were crushed out by her remorseless ambition, by her determination to go on with her life work. He flung himself angrily into his bachelor apartments. She was unworthy of any further thought, and that was the end of it. She was cold, she did not love him; at least he tried to persuade himself that was true, but he failed. His better self told him how utterly absurd it was to lay the blame on that. She did love him and he knew it. She loved him. He thought of the days, now so long gone by, when they had lived for nothing better than each other's presence. The recollection of it all filled him with a half-painful, half-pleasurable thrill. Well, there was no use thinking over the past; she might love him, but she was utterly incapable of making sacrifices for him. She loved herself better than him.

He sat a long time, in his big armchair, trying to put himself in her place. He thought over his own strong hopes and ambitious plans for the future, he reflected what it would mean to him to give up his profession, to sink his whole past with its memories, to give up his Lawyer's Club, his speech before the Society for Municipal Purity that very night; to renounce all his congenial associates, to sink all his dearest interests and go into some humdrum business. He began to have some faint conception of Helen's position, began to appreciate what he was demanding of her. Hers was no ordinary woman's fad; she did not take up her profession in that half-hearted, dilettante fashion as so many women did. And why did they? Because they believed marriage would put an end to it, and they hated to give up their hopes of married life. It certainly was natural that such an attitude should interfere with their earnestness in taking up a profession as an end in itself. Could he have worked so hard, so faithfully, had marriage appeared to him as a wall looming up in the future cutting off every other interest, every other ambition? Marriage, to him, had always meant renewed effort, a greater stimulus for success

A little reflection and Harold was able to forget a great deal of his bitterness toward Helen. He could even sympathize with her, he could—what could he do? Go back and say, "Take me, only marry me, and let me share a small part of your heart. Let me come in for a portion of your interest, side by side with your practice, your hospital, your scientific researches." Could he do that? Would any man? Impossible! It might be very hard on women, it might be unjust (he was almost ready to admit it) that they should have to make such a painful decision between their love and their ambition, their heart and their brain; but what could he do? How could he help it? Were not men and women born to marry? Had not one or the other to give up outside interests? how else could a home be made; a family reared? Could it be that it was the duty of the husband to remain home and take care of the cradle and socks, while the wife attended to her professional duties? The world might be awry; he was sorry for it, but would it be any less so if the men bore the brunt of it?

Suppose he let the future take care of itself? Suppose he defied it and reached forth his hands to grasp all that the present contained for him of joy and happiness? Suppose he forgot Helen, the physician; Helen, with her theories; Helen, with her ambitions; suppose he only remembered Helen, the woman; Helen, with the white skin; Helen, with the red lips; Helen with the bright, blue eyes? Only remembered his passionate desire to close all arguments with kisses, to crush her in his arms and feel her palpitating against him? Well, and what then? Suppose he subdued her? Suppose she yielded to him, what would the future have in store for them both? Would they be able to crush those terrible moments which would be sure to follow, moments when everyday life would interpose with thoughts of life's earnest duties, of duties forgotten, of powers wasted? There could be nothing but final misery to them, unless marriage could mean between them a long life of sympathetic friendship, of self-respect; a union with the consciousness of duty performed.

To accept from a woman the sacrifice of her professional life is almost as dangerous to future happiness as to accept from her the sacrifice of her honor. Helen had once said:

"Harold, if you conquer, and I marry you with your present ideas of woman's duties, if that means I am to give up my whole professional ambition, my sense of what I owe it and the world, if I am to sink my whole existence into being your wife, I shall feel degraded. I shall feel as much so as if I had lost the respect of the world. It would mean to me the victory of passion over reason, of my inclinations over my sense of duty. If I could honestly bring myself to believe that a woman's proper field is marriage, and that every other object in life ought to be waived for that, it would be easy for me. But I cannot. I have accomplished enough in my work to justify me in feeling that I have a mission, a duty to perform; to give this all up for you, is to make myself fall utterly in my eyes, and I could never be happy without the respect of my own self. To me it is more important than the respect of all the rest of the world."

He could understand this, as if he gave up his profession and all his higher instincts to follow in the footsteps of some frivolous courtesan, as if he had allowed his love to swallow up every other sentiment that a man is capable of cherishing. Well, it was hard on her, it was hard on him. It was too bad that life was not so constituted that two such people could marry, neither one giving up the necessary intellectual life, each separate, independent, yet united, blest with, love and all else besides that makes life worth living.

IV

Dr. Brent stood a moment before entering the great door of the Root Memorial Hospital. Glancing at the noble cluster of buildings she could not repress a sigh of mingled contentment and relief. It was almost fairyland to her; it meant the realization of her most dearly cherished dream.

To begin with, there was the college, which not only ranked with any medical college in the country, but did away with a great deal of the necessity of going abroad for the higher scientific training. The staff of instructors included many of the most noted specialists of the day. Among the envious or scoffing there was a good deal of fun poked at the "importations" for the great Root Memorial, for there were a number of German and Swedish professors, all of them members of the sterner sex. The Root Memorial was really founded to advance the medical education of women, not to provide for them remunerative positions, but to give them the very best instruction that could be had, so Dr. Brent did not believe in the necessity for women professors, and preferred to have the best irrespective of sex. For this she was severely censured by many, who said they thought the Root Memorial was to be a "College for Women." No one admired her own sex more than Dr. Brent; she thought they had done grandly considering the meager opportunities for study that had been granted them in the past. But that did not mean that they had received sufficient training to be already foremost in every department of learning, especially in one that requires so much training as medicine. There was quite a little passage at arms between Dr. Brent and Miss Keating, of Kansas (or rather I should have said her friends, who seemed more indignant than the abused party herself), because Miss Keating, the glory of Kansas, was asked to be an assistant to Professor Herrgoberger in the chemical laboratory. Miss Keating, an assistant, indeed! There were not lacking plenty of people to say that Dr. Brent was jealous of the rest of her own sex.

But all this small talk was a matter of complete indifference to Helen. How could she have room to consider such petty annoyances when she had so much to be really thankful for and so much demand for active work? In the college building were superbly equipped laboratories; a student could take a full course in chemistry, physics, botany, and zoology, and there were separate laboratories where really advanced work was encouraged. There were fellowships in abundance, and everything possible was done to foster the sentiment that the regulation three years did not mean the end of all study, and that the study of medicine did not necessarily mean merely preparation for active practice. It was Dr. Brent's great hope to instill into America something of the German love of science for itself, of a life spent in investigation, calm, slow, patient, but thorough, and culminating often in really great discoveries.

In the hospital were all the latest improvements; everything that could in any way promote the comfort of the patients or supplement the skill of the physician. Besides the college and the hospital, there was the training school for nurses adjoining. It was a homelike place, and everything possible was done to make the lives of the nurses pleasant and domestic. There was a committee interested in the training school, which did splendid work among the poorer quarters, trying to impress among the many poorly paid, overworked shopwomen the advantages of adopting the profession of trained nurse, but strange to say it was hard work to persuade that class of women that there was not something essentially immoral in the calling.

Indeed, Helen had cause to stand proudly before the magnificent buildings. Her three years since the laying of the cornerstone had been well spent. It had been a fearful strain. Mrs. Root was not satisfied unless every detail was supervised by Dr. Brent. First there had come up the question of selecting from the vast numbers of plans that had come in during the competition, which was open to all. The choice had fallen upon a well-known architect established in his profession many years; a man! and thereby Helen had called down upon herself a shower of criticism. She had actually rejected the plans of a woman architect! Many women had thought it outrageous that the competition should be open to men; this was to be a woman's hospital, and it ought to be used to advance women in every way. This and the famous Keating controversy before mentioned spread abroad the general impression that Dr. Brent was not really interested in the progress of her sex, and there were not a few that were quite ready to affirm that she was jealous of the success attained by any woman other than herself. We must not be too hard upon Helen's critics. Her faith to the trust to make the Root Memorial the best of its kind naturally met with little sympathy from such women as had swelled themselves with pride and gratification at the chance of really shutting out their opponents, the men. There was held a large meeting of a well-known Women's Club at which a radiant prophet had drawn a picture of what the Root Memorial would mean to women. It is almost unnecessary to add that it was a picture which drew forth rapturous applause.

First, there would be superb buildings designed by a woman architect; then there would be the hospital managed entirely by a board of women directors—even the treasurer would be a woman (and the speaker made highly felicitous and original allusion to the woman treasurer who would not be so apt to take sudden excursions into Canada); the doctors would be women, even from internes to consulting physicians, and the operations all by women surgeons. There would be no man cooks. She didn't know but that a capable janitress might do away with the usual incapable and shiftless janitor. But the climax was reached with the description of the college—a college wherein the very best instruction could be obtained by women. Where not only the students, but all the instructors would be women. Who dared deny that such women existed? Was there not the renowned Miss Keating and hosts of others nearly her equal?

That meeting was voted by all the most successful ever held. Fancy the chagrin when Dr. Brent not only refused to accept honorary membership extended by the club, but announced the plan of the institution in a prominent magazine and publicly deplored that kind of sentimentality which, actuated by an emotional, unreasoning love of Woman (always with a capital W), was fascinated by the magic name and was blinded to what really makes for the best interests not only of Woman, but of humanity. Dr. Brent had a contempt for that sort of sexual rivalry that goes on so bitterly among a certain class of women, that kind of rivalry which is so ardent that faults as well as virtues are copied in the eager race after similitude.

It is impossible to relate all the numerous wearisome struggles which Helen had to undergo with this form of sentimentality in woman. In truth Helen was broad, in a way in which very few women are broad; restrictions and forced limitations had failed to embitter her. She still cared more for the development of humanity than for the development of woman, more for the progress of civilization than for the progress of a certain portion of it. She believed that every real and earnest advance made by women must mean real advance made by the entire world, but it must *be real advance.* I am almost afraid to say it, for I naturally want my heroine to be popular, but I suspect Helen was really more interested in the fact that the Root Memorial Hospital and College would advance the condition of medical preparation all over the country, in the fact that it encouraged original research, and inculcated the love of science, for science's sake, not for breadwinning only; I suspect very strongly that she cared more for the Root Memorial because it accomplished all this, than (dare I breathe it?) merely because it was another college open to women without restrictions. In fact the board of trustees was soon earnestly discussing the question of opening the college to men students, as numerous applications had been made. Dr. Brent's critics were busy making up their minds whether to be most tickled at the thought of men applying for admission to a woman's college, or indignant that the policy of retaliation would not be pursued. But again Helen's interest in humanity, rather than in Woman, showed itself. If the Root Memorial did stand for something not elsewhere obtainable, if its greatness was felt so strongly as to make men beg for its privileges, why surely to deny their entrance would be to deprive a large part of humanity from a great source of growth. It would be a cheap kind of revenge, while the granting of the request would be a sublime move onward.

Fortunate it was for Helen that her life was so full of duties that there had been no time to repine or to reflect bitterly upon the past. She could not shut out the memory of Harold from her heart, do what she would, but then it was a great blessing to have a rich, full life—not that for a moment she ever deceived herself into believing it was a complete life. She often thought she could never have borne her decision had she been an author or a poet, had she not thrown herself, heart and soul, into the profession that takes one most out of one's self. What a deep pity she felt for Aurora, "laboring on alone."

> To sit alone,
> And think for comfort, how that very night,
> Affianced lovers, leaning face to face
> With sweet half-listenings for each other's breath,
> Are reading haply from some page of ours.

There was not much "sitting alone" for busy Dr. Brent. Professional calls, grave operations, tri-weekly lectures, board meetings, committee meetings, meetings of the dozens of societies to which she belonged, work in the laboratory and the reading of, and writing for medical journals, left little time for such thoughts. She was in the rush, the stress, the whirl of life; not a day passed without its demand upon her active sympathies, upon her hand, her brain, and her heart. Did she regret the great decision that had shaped her life? Regret? No, not in the sense that she would she had done differently. There was a regret, however, a deep-seated, passionate regret that such a struggle of the dual nature of woman should ever be necessary. There was within her a fierce longing that her whole nature could rise and expand, grow as it was intended it should grow—full, proportioned, equable, beautifully rich in all the blessings of life; not warped, thwarted, stunted, as she could not but realize it was. And yet, what was there to be done? Could she ever have been happy had her decision been different? She knew that life was not complete to her, but she also knew it would have been far less complete, less satisfying, had she subdued the intellectual rather than the emotional side of her nature. No, there was absolutely nothing for women to do to help on the solution of this great problem of marriage. The change must come from men. They must be educated to allow greater liberty of thought and action in their wives, to seek in them companionship in marriage, to seek sympathetic co-operation, not merely physical gratification, nor the mere oiling of the household machinery.

Dr. Brent delivered her lecture on gynecology and then stepped into one of the chemical laboratories. There she found a young girl bending over her desk, evidently deeply absorbed in the experiment she was carrying on. A handsome young German professor stood watching the scene. He came up to Helen—

"Pardon me, but Fräulein Bayley is killing herself. I can never get her to go home at reasonable hours to her meals."

The young girl looked up, with a bright laugh. Her face was not beautiful, but it was full of enthusiasm and earnestness. Helen smiled.

"Come, Lotus, dear, it is time to go home. Moderation is your first duty. Remember you ruin the cause of your entire sex if you break down in the midst of your experiments. All the world will pat itself on the back and say, 'Aha, did we not always say women were not fit for chemistry?'"

Lotus hastily washed some glasses, put away her instruments in her desk, rushed for her cloak and her hat, and soon was accompanying Helen to their home.

V

Lotus Bayley lived with Helen, and they were deeply attached to one another. Lotus's mother had been one of Dr. Brent's most fashionable patients. One day she brought Lotus to the office.

"Doctor," she said. "My daughter here is killing herself."

Dr. Brent looked at the well rounded figure and the bright, gray eyes of the daughter and smiled.

"Really," protested the mother. "She is very headstrong and she will persist in going on with those ridiculous studies of hers. Just as if a daughter of mine has any need to be poring over her books all day!"

The doctor passed one quiet, sympathetic look upon the young girl, a look that won her at once.

"Of what does she complain?" she asked, with a slight emphasis on the pronoun.

Mrs. Bayley blushed faintly, and replied with some heat, "Why, she doesn't eat well, and she's growing round shouldered and pale, and she doesn't get time to see any of her friends."

"Quite a category of complaints. May I ask you, Mrs. Bayley, does your daughter attend gymnasium?"

Lotus gave a sudden, grateful look, which lit up her large gray eyes.

"Gymnasium, doctor? Great Heavens! I have come to you to make her do less, and now you actually suggest something else."

"Why, it does not seem to me that college can possibly take up all her time." Lotus now spoke for herself:

"Mother, we ought to tell the doctor of our compromise. When mother permitted me to attend college, I, on my part, promised to take embroidery lessons every day, and not to neglect my calls." Mrs. Bayley looked just a little foolish.

"Well, you couldn't expect me to consent to her being brought up like a heathen." Dr. Brent looked grave, then taking Lotus's hand in hers, and drawing the young girl up to her, she said:

"Mrs. Bayley, you must pardon me if I seem abrupt. I think you know me well enough to know that I do not often lecture. Permit me, this once, however, to speak my mind frankly." Mrs. Bayley nodded; Lotus stared. The doctor continued: " I have had brought to me any number of cases of nervous prostration. Very few of these have been brought about by over-study. In fact, I may say really none of them have been so brought about. I have, on the contrary, seen hundreds of cases where the breakdown has been caused by over-dissipation. I have seen pneumonias resulting from the absurdly inadequate clothing of the fashionable evening world; I have seen severe anaemia resulting from irregular hours and consequent loss of sleep; I have seen many other troubles brought on by the constant strain that social duties lay upon the entire nervous system. I have also had many mothers bring me what they called cases of over-study. For these, however, there have generally been quite other causes for the breakdown than the one given. I shall explain. You allow your eldest daughter, Rose, to enter society in full swing. You are pleased if she enters it body and soul. If she has been up late the night before, you permit her to sleep well into the day. If she is tired from the waltz, you are glad if she will rest upon the sofa until it is time for her to dress for a luncheon or a tea. If she has young friends with whom she is congenial you seek to bring her in contact with them. Everything is done to make her surroundings congenial and to smooth the difficulties in her path. You will pardon me if I say that the same consideration is rarely shown to the daughter that goes to college. If, after a struggle, she finally succeeds in securing the consent of her parents, she goes, indeed, but everything is done to make her feel that she has done something out of the way; that she is, in fact, an abnormal creature to prefer books and learning to society and pleasure. Is she permitted to throw herself heart and soul into her life, as her sister into hers? On the contrary, is there not usually a constant friction going on at home? If she wishes to pass the evening quietly in her room studying (a pastime which is not half so dreadful as it is made out, not half so dangerous to health as dancing half-naked in the ballroom) she is not only supposed to be killing herself with over-work, but is gently reminded that her dreadful, studious ways are breaking up the life of the family. Life of the family, indeed! How much is there of it, I should like to know, when like as not, on descending to the parlor, our student finds some visitor chatting idly and insipidly with the elder sister, while all the others sit around and pretend not to be bored. Why must all the life of the family center about the society girl? Why must our tired mothers be dragged to the ball to watch over dear Aurelia? why must the entire family be made uncomfortable in some over-crowded summer hotel because it is the fashion and dear Aurelia must be in the swim? Why, there would be absolutely no girls in college to-day, if their going made one-third the commotion that is made by the girl going out into society. What are we to judge from all this? I am afraid nothing else than, that the sole end of a girl's existence is to make a brilliant match, and that a girl who is foolish or whimsical enough to care for any other end of existence must be put down, and reminded at every turn how foolish she is and how much more rational and affable and womanly is her sister.

"Well, Mrs. Bayley, this is quite a long lecture, much longer than I had originally intended. I am afraid I got too much warmed up with my subject. Now let me prescribe for your daughter, for after all that is what you came for, and not to listen to a lecture by me. Well, I shall write you one." The doctor turned to her desk, and wrote for a few moments, then turning to Mrs. Bayley, she handed her a bit of folded paper upon which was written the prescription. Mrs. Bayley opened it and read:

R Loose, sensible, plain gowns.

Gymnasium at least twice weekly.

Horseback or bicycle tri-weekly for an hour in morning, after light breakfast.

Early hours for retiring.

Liberty to seek the quiet of her room, if desired.

Liberty to seek the companionship of her classmates.

VI

It was not very long after Lotus's introduction to Helen that the engagement of her pretty sister, Rose, was announced. Rose was the heroine of the hour. She had secured "the greatest catch in town," and she attained to that great height of feminine grandeur—to be envied by everyone of her bosom friends. There had been some unkind rumors to the effect that Rose had been in love with a struggling young lawyer, who had since gone West, but surely that was only the revenge of some of the envious ones. Who could have hesitated between being plain Mrs. John Brown, with five thousand a year, or Mrs. Mortimer Stuart Verplanck with $250,000 a year?

To begin with, the Verplanck family had led the wealth and fashion of the metropolis for generations and generations, and the Stuart family was connected very directly with—, who signed the Declaration of Independence. Signed the Declaration of Independence, indeed? Independence from what? From snobbery? Has anyone ever reflected upon the irony of fate in this modern pride in claiming kinship to some signer of the Declaration of Independence? That boasted ancestor affixed his name in approval of a sentiment that "All men are created equal," and with the last flourish of his pen he innocently and unconsciously conferred upon all of his descendants the "inalienable right" to turn up their aristocratic noses at those lesser mortals that had been unequally created without such distinguished forefathers.

Then, Mortimer's sister had married an English lord, and Lady Milminme was now the acknowledged belle of London

society. Think of the advantage of being received in London as
the sister-in-law of the beautiful Lady Milminme and of being
entertained at her sumptuous mansion! Can the eloquent pen of
the novelist add more to uphold the importance, the fame, the
glory of the marriage about to be consummated? Is not everyone
of my female readers worked up to the proper pitch of enthusiasm,
or will it be necessary for me to add the final touch and state that
it was rumored that Lady Milminme's wedding gift to her future
sister would be a dinner service in solid gold, and that, owing to
the high position of Lord Milminme, the Queen had signified her,
intention of sending a diamond brooch to the young bride?

I am obliged to reluctantly confess (for, as I have said
before, I want my heroine to be popular) that Helen failed to
be impressed. I am afraid she would have stood firmly beyond
the reach of the most eloquent pen ever possessed by novelist's
cunning. What was a greater test: she stood the fire of Mrs.
Bayley's eloquence expatiating upon the blissful happiness that
had befallen her daughter. Think of resisting the eloquence of a
proud mamma, whose eldest is about to marry the wealthiest and
handsomest bachelor in New York, the most graceful leader in the
german, and—not to be forgot—the brother of Lady Milminme.
Her daughter was to marry a man who possessed all these rare and
varied qualities that bespoke him a good, devoted and faithful
husband, and Helen refused to be impressed. It was cruel. The
end of it was, Mrs. Bayley went over to the camp of Dr. Thaddeus
Manning. I must also reluctantly confess—it is always hard to
make such a confession, but conscience demands it—that this
time my heroine was wrong. It was foolish and willful in her to be
blind to all the advantages about to be possessed by the fortunate
Rose. But Helen was a physician, we must remember, and she

was apt to prize health and strength above all things. And she had
warned Mrs. Bayley that Rose might be preparing for herself a
very much more miserable future than merely not having enough
ball dresses or not possessing a house for the London season. To
Dr. Brent, Mortimer Stuart Verplanck was not the handsomest
man in New York. He was not handsome at all. In her professional
eyes, beauty meant health, and health was one of the last qualities
with which Dr. Brent would have credited Mortimer Stuart
Verplanck.

The day of the marriage was fast approaching; each great
daily was vying with the other to secure the most accurate
description of the great affair, the most complete list of the guests,
and the most detailed account of the wedding presents.

One day Helen sat in her office, completely tired out. She
was generally cheerful and strong, but this day she was not only
utterly tired, but discouraged, for she had been hunting for a good
nurse for one of her patients upon whom she had lately laid the
crown of motherhood. It was always a discouraging task to her
because of the numbers of miserable women whom she had to
interview and the tales of misery she was obliged to listen to. All
this crushed her with a keen sense of the misery upon earth, of the
injustice of the social standard of morals and her own slight power
to remedy it. On this particular day she had examined woman after
woman and had been unable to secure what she wanted. It was late
in the afternoon when the doorbell rang and a young girl timidly
entered the office. Helen scarcely looked up; she was merely aware
that it was a woman without a baby. She asked wearily:

"Where is your baby? I am sick of wasting so much time. I
told them at the office not to send any more women unless they
brought their babies. You know it is absolutely essential that I

examine the baby. Go back and get it and then I'll see you!" The answer came low and hesitating:

"I didn't know."

"Is your baby alive?"

"No, ma'am."

"Humph! That won't do at all. How long did it live?"

"It didn't live at all, ma'am."

"Then you certainly will not do," and Helen leaned back and sighed in a discouraged way. The girl turned away and half fell, half leaned against a seat, exclaiming below her breath:

"Good Lord, what will become of me?"

Helen jumped up and ran to the girl. If she had not been so thoroughly dispirited she never would have permitted her to go without a kind word, without endeavoring in some way to assist her. Now as she looked closely at the girl she noticed the fair skin, the pretty, soft, blond hair that told of former beauty, and the hollow cheeks and sunken eyes that told of present ill-health and misery. "The old, old story," Helen muttered between her teeth. She drew the girl to her sympathetically, and softly spoke a few words of comfort. The girl continued to cry in a dull, hopeless sort of way:

"This is the third refusal I've had to-day. Nobody wants me because my baby didn't live. It wasn't my fault."

"Probably not," muttered Helen.

"I have no place to go and I don't know what will become of me."

Helen patted her hand. "Come, come, we'll get something for you to do. I never failed yet; but my poor girl," she added, looking sharply at her, "the place for you, just now, is the hospital. You mustn't think of taking any position until you are better."

Helen remained closeted with the girl a long time. Then she called a cab and drove with her to the hospital. She was put into Dr. Brent's own service. That night Helen found little sleep. She paced up and down, up and down, with anger and hesitation. A tragic story had been revealed to her, but that was not the worst of it. A doctor, especially a woman doctor, becomes accustomed to these experiences, if she takes any pains to go among the miserable of her sex. And with Helen this was her greatest work. Never was she more really content with herself than when she was about it. But in this case the cruelty of the social structure of morals was brought before her with particular violence. Here in the hospital now lay a woman whose future was utterly wrecked, whose physical condition was utterly ruined, who, if possibly spared to life, would have no future, no outlook, who would be shunned and pitied (that would be far too mild a word), and the father of her child, where was he? No doubt sitting at this moment in one of the most elegant houses on Fifth Avenue, his arms about a young girl, who was about to unite her fresh, innocent life with his, who yet would have shrunk in horror and disgust from this poor, ruined woman. And what could Dr. Brent do? What could she accomplish, single-handed, against the whole world? Suppose she were to stand on the housetops and proclaim the story to all. What would that world say? Why, merely that it was very poor taste in Dr. Brent to say all this just while the preparations for the marriage were going on. Why could she not have waited? Waited! That was just what she did not want to do. Wait! Wait until her little friend was bound to this man. Oh, yes; what else was there to do? Suppose she told, would it influence the mother, who was bent upon the match? Did her revelation affect the social position of the man? Did what she had to say have any importance? Any bearing upon the question at hand? Did she come to prove that he was not the brother of a member of the English aristocracy? Did she come to prove that he did not possess an income of $250,000 a year? Ah, if that had been her message she knew she would have been well received and heeded. Had it any importance, any consequence? Ah, yes; surely what she had to tell was of more than ordinary importance. It was more than a tale of the so-called ordinary social peccadillos. What Dr. Brent had before suspected was now but too plain. This greatest catch in New York had no right to enter upon the duties of a husband and a father.

If she were to come to the mother with a tale of approaching disease, of some illness, subtle but sure, that was going to attack her daughter, would not the mother listen?

VII

Mrs. Bayley was at home and seemed surprised to see Helen, with well-bred surprise—just a slight elevation of her eyebrows and a polite expression about being so honored by the visit of such a very much engaged woman. But Helen was too earnest to remain long chatting about social nothings, and Mrs. Bayley seemed to catch something of her earnestness and began to look somewhat nervous. Helen asked to be taken into the private boudoir, where they would be free from interruption. They had a long talk.

"I am surprised at you," finally broke in Mrs. Bayley, "I thought you were more a woman of the world, doctor, than to ask me to do such a preposterous thing as to break off the match at this late day. Why, what news have you told me? Now, my dear doctor, you don't really think that I have thought a handsome young fellow with such an enormous fortune could very well have lived the life of a saint? If I listened to you I might as well make up my mind, once for all, to have my daughters remain old maids to the end of their days."

Helen spoke eloquently for a few moments.

"But, my dear doctor," interrupted Mrs. Bayley. "Who knows the girl isn't lying? Shall I ruin my daughter's happiness, her future—"

"Ah, there we have it," thought Helen.

"For the sake of a few idle words spoken by a disappointed and wretched girl? How do we know that she really came from a respectable family in the country? How do we know anything about it?"

"No, my dear woman" thought Helen. "You will be careful to know as little as possible about it."

"You say, yourself, the girl is hardly accountable for what she says. You admit to me that she is at this moment delirious with high fever. How, then, can you expect me to ruin my poor child's career, to make a public scandal which might kill her, all for this silly, irresponsible girl?"

"Very well, call her silly and irresponsible. Who has made her so? You are afraid to kill your child by breaking off this match, by the publicity of the scandal. If that is what you are really afraid of I shall tell you what you force me to say, which I am sorry is necessary for me to say. You are finding a very much surer way to kill your daughter than by breaking off this match."

Mrs. Bayley looked startled, "Why, what do you mean?"

Helen flushed deeply. Then she spoke for some minutes, so low that Mrs. Bayley could scarcely catch her words. This time the shot did not go astray. Mrs. Bayley's fat face paled. For a few moments there was dead silence, and Helen's heart beat with hope. Finally Mrs. Bayley rose and, in a broken voice, she incoherently muttered something; Helen could just make out the words:

"Doctors sometimes mistaken—think they know everything—change of habits—marriage—my poor girl—new life—reformation," etc.

By this time Helen realized that her effort had been indeed futile. She left the house, wise in the knowledge of how far a mother's ambition will permit her to go.

The wedding took place. It was the grandest, the most magnificent affair of the season. The papers gave more space to

it than if it had been the founding of a new college or the death
of a great genius. It was solemnized in church, the bishop himself
officiating. The flowers were superb, the music heavenly, the
wedding jewels queenly. Helen was forced to hear from all her
patients how beautiful it had been, what magnificent presents had
been sent, what a great success it was, how the caterer had made a
reputation for himself at the breakfast, and how pretty and happy
the bride had looked. Well, *if ever* a girl had everything to be happy
for, it was Rose.

VIII

The honeymoon was a delightful one. Rose had a trip to Europe. She had her visit to Lady Milminme—a visit which was all a dream of delight; and she had been presented at one of the Queen's drawing rooms, and Her Majesty had smiled with particular affability, as she recognized her own gift sparkling upon the young bride's shoulder. There had been the excitement of designing the great presentation costume which all had concurred in pronouncing a striking success; there had been the satisfaction of reading about herself, her social triumphs, her latest gowns, the entertainments given in her honor, etc., in the society columns of the papers forwarded her from home.

Then there was the season at Lady Milminme's country seat. Grey Oaks, the fascinating, old-fashioned, ancestral home of the Milminme family for generations past. It was all like the pages from some old novel. Rose could have continued her European stay forever, it seemed to her, but she found she had to return to America sooner than she had anticipated. She naturally wished to be with her mother.

Then came a dreary time of wretchedness, when she hung her head and did not much care whether life went on or not. It was a dull succession of days and days of discomfort and misery. Besides, she hated Dr. Manning, but beg as she would, her mother was unmoved and Dr. Brent was not sent for. One day there came a great stillness into the great house. No one spoke above a whisper; the servants went about their duties, to and fro, on tiptoe. But there was lacking the sly smile peeping out amidst all the anxiety, there was lacking the half-hidden, half-hushed joy, there were absent the tender little sounds from the sickroom, the helpless little wailings—all that never came. It was soon whispered abroad that Rose's child had never lived, that it was a half-formed little creature and was buried quickly.

Rose grew very ill, the doctor shook his head, there were consultations after consultations. Still Rose begged for Helen, and at last her mother gave way and she was sent for. Dr. Manning was only too glad to hand over his patient to Dr. Brent's care. He knew he was being relieved from having a death on his hands. He had small hopes; Helen had none. She watched day and night, but her devotion was of no avail. It was too late before she was sent for; Rose's condition had been past help.

When Helen stood over Rose's body she felt like a murderer. How much more cause had the mother to feel so. Helen felt small pity for the now completely broken woman, who hysterically reiterated that she had killed her only child, her only child. Helen had tried soothing, and now she endeavored to quiet the woman with sterner methods.

"Madam, tears and wailing will not bring back your daughter, nor have you any right to speak as if she were your only child. You still have another daughter and your duty is to live for her."

Mrs. Bayley continued to sob bitterly, "Oh, yes; I have a daughter, but she can't be mine. Sometimes I wonder where she came from, she's so different from poor Rose. She never loved me; she isn't like my own flesh and blood. I can't bear to think she has been spared, while my poor Rose has been taken away, I could hate Lotus for living."

It was too late, there stood Lotus in the doorway, grasping the portiere; she looked the picture of desolation.

It was after that, Lotus had taken up her home with Helen.

IX

Mrs. Keith-Brew's parlors were crowded. Cards had been sent out (or a tea and all tier friends turned out in force—not to see her, but to see her friends and to take note of all the beautiful things their hostess had brought home on her latest return from abroad. The rooms were brilliantly lighted and the busy buzz of voices would have been simply maddening to anyone inexperienced enough to stop in one's conversation to listen to the confusion of sounds. The only safe-guard against distraction at such a place is to plunge into conversation and forget what goes on about you. One must bend one's entire energies to the noble task of listening to the voice of the nearest neighbor.

Mrs. Keith-Brew and her two daughters stand valiantly at the door and have been standing on that identical spot for the past two hours. This is seeing one's dear friends in New York. They will stand there smiling and bowing for one hour more and then they will be released. Mrs. Keith-Brew is a fine looking woman of something over forty. Her daughters have very little to say for themselves; she has a good deal to say, and makes up for their silence. She is particularly fond of telling all her friends how miserable she was before she went abroad and how wonderfully she had been cured by Dr. Brent. She is talking on her favorite subject now, to a slender, beautiful woman with soft auburn hair and sparkling black eyes, who is noticeably the most elegantly dressed woman in the room.

"I assure you, my dear," she is saying. "There is positively no one like her. You know they do say Dr. Manning is wild with jealously. She takes half his practice away. And then, you know, there's that hospital, the one founded by that awful Mrs. Root."

"With the fearful dyed hair, and the dowdy camel's-hair shawl?"

"The very same—Oh, how do you do, Mr. Watts, I am so glad to see you. My daughters, Mr. Watts—What, Miss Sprague, not going to take any tea? Such a very cold day—And as I was saying. Dr. Manning was furious when I left him—How good of you to have come, dear Mrs. Morse—And Dr. Brent did me worlds of good, as you see."

"Just fancy, a woman physician; my husband is so prejudiced against them."

"Why, you don't tell me! But then no one could dislike Dr. Brent. Why this is too sweet of you, doctor, in the midst of all your work; I was just singing your praises and I have made this lady quite wild to meet you. Dr. Brent, let me introduce you to Mrs. Skidmore, Mrs. Harold Skidmore—Ah, so Mr. Pratt, you did come, after all your abuse of teas?"

"Mrs. Skidmore."

"Dr. Brent."

"You fool," shrieks a tall woman, into Mrs. Keith-Brew's ear. "Didn't you know—" the rest is lost; Mrs. Keith-Brew turns with an exclamation of dismay. Dr. Brent smiles, perfectly self-possessed.

"I wonder if he has told her," quickly went through her mind.

"Indeed, doctor, you have a very doughty champion in our hostess and I am so very glad to meet you. Of course I have heard any amount about you. I have had quite a curiosity. Mr. Skidmore, you know, or perhaps you don't know, is most obstinately set against women becoming physicians. It's too absurd; he is really quite broad-minded in many things, but then that is one of his hobbies, I suppose, so I must put up with it."

"He has not told her," concluded Dr. Brent.

"Why, how are you, Mrs. Skidmore," exclaims a pert little lady, interrupting and talking very fast. "And where is Mr. Skidmore, isn't he going to honor us to-day, or does he look down upon us little mortals who have time to attend teas? It would be such a pleasure now for me to see my name to-morrow right after that of the Honorable Harold Skidmore."

"You will have to be contented with his wife," Mrs. Skidmore answered.

"Oh, no," exclaimed someone. "He'll be here anyway, according to to-morrow's papers."

Helen was about to slip off, but she was seized.

"Now, Dr. Brent," exclaimed the same indefatigable talker. "This is too bad! Mrs. Skidmore was just saying we should not have the honor of having Mr. Skidmore and now you want to desert us. We must really keep one celebrity, you know. You don't appreciate, Mrs. Skidmore, what a compliment the doctor is paying us in coming at all. She rarely if ever attends such frivolous things as teas."

"But the mandates of Mrs. Keith-Brew are not to be defied."

"No, indeed; but tell us what horrible operation have you had on hand this afternoon, and to what terrible scene of misery are you now wending your footsteps. I am sure it will be something horrible as a sort of penance for having been frivolous here."

Here a young fellow came up to Mrs. Skidmore, and Helen could not but listen with interest.

"Oh, come now, Mrs. Skidmore, it's too bad of your husband to treat us so. He makes a young, struggling lawyer like myself feel ashamed of being here. I feel as if I, too, ought to have a hundred and forty cases weighing on my conscience, and a dozen trips to Albany and Washington. It's too bad of him, really."

Mrs. Skidmore smiled. She seemed pleased at the unusual notice that was taken of her husband's absence.

"Yes," she assented," Mr. Skidmore has little time for any pleasures and I must serve as a substitute, although a very poor one, I know. He never goes out socially in the afternoons, and even in the evenings half the time I am all dressed, waiting for him, when a telegram comes to me saying, 'I am unavoidably detained,' or 'Called suddenly to Washington, back in three days.' It's a horrid profession."

"That is the punishment of being the wife of Harold Skidmore."

Helen turned away and sought to find her hostess's nieces, who were presiding over the tea table. She wanted to get out of the crowd. The silly nothings of conversation, the whole atmosphere of hollowness, of glitter, of insincerity, she longed to escape from as soon as possible. She was conscious that her hopes, her aims, her theory of life were so irrevocably different from those of the women about her. She did not often attend teas, and when she was obliged to do so, she returned to her home tired and out of sorts. She always refreshed herself with the biography of some great woman. She would take down some volume from her shelf and enjoy a peaceful reading of the career of Dorothea Dix, or Mary Somerville, or Margaret Fuller; of some woman that had nobly lived up to some definite purpose, some great life work. She required these moments to bring back her damaged faith in womanhood. It was like breathing the fresh air of the fields after the heavy atmosphere of the crowded parlor

She struggled through the crowd. At one time she found herself in the midst of a chattering group of ladies. The topic of conversation was so interesting to her, that she was forced, almost in spite of herself, to stand still and listen with a sort 'of fascination, painful as it was. One lady was saying:

"Well, now, that's very well, Mrs. Parker, but my husband is a minister and you can have no idea what that means."

Several ladies murmured their sympathy.

"To begin with, I never dare go near him, and the children, good gracious, they mustn't speak above a whisper, while he is preparing a sermon, and Sunday instead of being a day of rest is his hardest day. He never has one blessed moment to himself, not one. And then all the week it's one thing after another. He doesn't have any time to know his own children, he's so constantly having to attend to other people's. Then there's his Bible class and the free school and the Society for the Prevention of Vice, and the Society for the Protection of Orphans. I do wish that someone would start a society for the Protection of Lone Minister's Wives."

There was a general laugh at this sally. Another broke in.

"But, my dear woman, confess, at least, that your husband has the best of it in the summer. There you go away together for a glorious summer jaunt, but as for my poor husband, he never gets off. We generally remain in town for some horribly late and unmethodical creature, and come flying back before half our vacation is over for some equally vexatious, over-impatient one."

"It's too bad, it is too bad," said someone. "They ought to arrange more considerately."

"It's perfectly frightful," she went on. "And last summer the doctor went to Europe with a patient. It sounds lovely, doesn't it? But I assure you, he came home thoroughly worn out and exhausted with his constant attendance, and I had a doleful enough summer in a horrid little hole all alone with the children."

"Well, maybe we do have it better in the summer," remarked the minister's wife. "But it makes up for it during the rest of the year, and mind you, a minister's wife does not dare look cross of out of temper, and mustn't say naughty things."

"Well, you get your meals straight, anyway," rejoined the other. "If it weren't for the children, I suppose we'd never sit down to a meal. He's never home on time, and as for keeping cooks— well, you know what that is, when one's meals are all topsy-turvy." Helen was about to pass on with a peculiar smile, when someone noticed her and called out:

"Ah, Dr. Brent, come here. We wives are holding an indignation meeting."

"Not that we blame our poor husbands in the least," hastened to add the two complainants deprecatingly.

"It's good you're not married," continued the person that had called to Dr. Brent. "We have just been hearing what frightful better-halves you doctors make." Helen answered in some heat (perhaps it did seem a little unwarranted, but then, how were they expected to understand?):

"Excuse me, Mrs. Smith, but it is only the men physicians that can afford to neglect their homes. There would be few women physicians if they married, and their better halves had to bear the burdens you are talking about. You see I was not fortunate enough to find any man that was sufficiently self-sacrificing to take irregular meals, and give up vacations for me, so I am left a forlorn old maid," and with a light laugh she passed on.

There was a rather startled pause.

"How changed she is; isn't it too bad how all these strong-minded women do get sour," someone said.

"Well, they do say, she had quite a romantic love story, you know," added another.

X

It was a great blessing to Helen to have Lotus, the young, enthusiastic girl in her home. It took a great loneliness away from Helen's heart and it forced her to hide many a discouragement and fit of depression. She could not bear to dim her young friend's bright horizon. But the night when Helen returned from Mrs. Keith-Brew's reception, the two began a discussion which drew Helen out in a way that she never intended. She had entered the study and found Lotus seated on a low stool by the fire. She had been reading Margaret Fuller's "Woman in the Nineteenth Century," and the book had dropped and lay upon the rug. She looked up thoughtfully as Helen entered.

"Helen," she said, dreamily, "I have found a motto for my life."

"Yes? What is it?"

"'I have always thought that the restraints upon the sex were insuperable only to those who think them so, or who noisily strive to break them.'"

"It is a bold motto."

"Yes, but it is true. I am going to do all I purpose and not go out of my sphere, nor force my way at all. A true woman can combine much."

"Yes, if she meets a man that will permit it."

Lotus blushed. She thought she knew one that would.

"You don't mean to tell me," she said, "she need to go into the kitchen and boil the egg herself."

"Don't ask me, little woman; I hate to discourage you."

"Oh, please don't treat me like a child. I want to know. I think you are bitter sometimes and try to hide it from me, dear. I don't mean to pry or to ask you anything you don't want to tell me, but I sometimes think something has happened in your life that makes you bitter on one subject, and that you are not your own dear, sweet self."

Helen stooped over and kissed the girl.

"Don't you think," Lotus went on. "Don't you think there are men, that believe their wives can be just as good and true wives and mothers without sewing every stitch for their children, or making every pie?"

"I know there are some—but they are few, very few."

"That is wrong. I am going to change all that. I am going to do my share, anyway, toward showing that women can direct and manage household affairs without getting buried in them and having no other outlook. I am going to give men a lesson right off. Helen, let me go to market for the future."

Helen laughed, "You must not make the mistake which many women make and cry out blindly against men. You must not lay all the blame upon them; my experience is, that women fail to understand us much more than men do."

"Oh, please don't tell me that."

"I am sorry, dear, but you will find it out for yourself, and have you not just told me not to treat you like a child? Of course it is easily accounted for. Women have lived so long in such a narrow sphere that their judgment is warped. They have become conservative through seeing only one phase of life; only one kind of existence going on. Men, on the contrary, through rubbing up against many men and women, through seeing so many phases of life, so many types of people, often acquire a breadth, even the most ordinary, uneducated men, which is not possessed by any but an exceptionally broad-minded woman."

"Yes; that is so."

"Then a happy woman seldom thinks any woman needs any different sphere than the one she herself so gracefully fills. You know what Hawthorne says, 'Women seldom disquiet themselves about the rights or wrongs of their sex, unless their own individual affections happen to lie in idleness or to be ill at ease.' Now this is not perfectly true, there are many women who are perfectly happy and have blessed lots that nevertheless do go forth and work for their sex. Still it is largely true that a happy wife who knows nothing out of her own narrow circle—and only a woman that has stood out in the world and worked can know how narrow that wife's sphere is—will toss her head and say, 'I want nothing better: motherhood is the crowning glory of woman's lot.' How can they know of the hundreds that can never wear that crown of glory; of the hundreds that wear it as a crown of—Oh, how can I talk to you, child, of these things?"

The girl had crept over to Helen and lay at her feet, holding her hands.

"Tell me, Helen, do not stop. I am not so young. I am anxious to learn, to know. Teach me to do right; teach me to do something for women to make them happy."

"You will need another teacher. Most women work for the happiness of others when they set about their philanthropic work. You may be surprised when I tell you that my chief aim in working is to make all women find themselves."

"Find themselves?"

"Yes; it may be a great deal to make them happy, but remember the words of Christ: 'For what shall a man be profited if he shall gain the whole world, and forfeit his soul?' Indeed, what is the good of material happiness, or where is the grace of marriage, no matter what comes with it, if the real soul be forfeited? The time came for me long ago, when I had to choose between losing or finding myself. Not that I really did find myself, but neither did I entirely lose myself. It is all wrong that so few women exist that have truly, in every sense of the word, found themselves; found their complete, rounded selves. What we must work for is the recognition of the true dignity of the individual. The rights of the individual genius must be recognized everywhere in man or woman, but they are not. You will answer incredulously, 'What, do we not now recognize genius, when we find it in either sex; have we not praised without stint George Eliot, for example; have we not placed her quite by the side of our great Thackeray?' As novelists, perhaps, but as individuals, surely not. Suppose Thackeray were to neglect his family sometimes and refuse to take his place in the bosom of his home circle; if he preferred to finish his 'Newcomes' or 'Pendennis,' who would have said one word in protest? And why is it that we are so proud that George Eliot knew how to make pies and put up jam? Why is it that some third-rate professor in some far-away Western 'university' will be the grand mogul of his family, must not be disturbed in his calculations, baby must stop crying, Mary Ann must cease rattling the dishes, his dinner must be kept nice and warm? But can a Mrs. Somerville dare these things? Do we not rather point with pride to the fact that she was the most exquisite of darners, made all her own dresses, and was ever ready to hide her manuscript under the table cover and smilingly receive the visits of the neighbors? Answer me, is this not the real tragedy of woman's lot to-day? One home neglected by a woman and the whole world is up in arms. A thousand homes neglected by the lord and master, and the world smiles and shrugs its shoulders. 'Que faire?' it says."

"But I suppose the man must be more leniently judged since it is he that must earn the bread and butter."

"Ah, yes; to be sure. The comfort and beauty of the home are to center about that one great fact. I scorn that view—but I won't even enter into that now. Will you tell me why the man has always to be the only bread earner? You will be shocked. 'What! can the woman earn her living and leave the baby?' But there are many ways of earning one's bread and butter. It often would not take her away from the baby more than cooking in the kitchen, and the additional money might enable her to keep a respectable nurse. How many homes have I seen where the wife is degraded into a second servant because the husband is too thin-skinned to permit her to earn any money. The world would think she is mistreated; that he does not earn enough for two, and ought not to have married. You see many a disagreeable task can be hidden at home in the nursery and in the kitchen, but why should not a woman have at least her choice? There are teaching and writing. Many things can be done that do not starve the mind and soul as does housework. How many men are broad-minded enough to permit their wives to have a Kindergarten or a little school in their parlors; how many would not insist that they be household drudges? It is simply conventionality. Somehow we don't look shocked when a fairly well-to-do man tells us with pride that his wife makes all the desserts and all the dresses for the children. Why then, under Heaven, should there be such a difference about confessing that one's wife teaches children or describes the fashions or illustrates books for a living?

"Many a broken-down woman comes to me for treatment, who is simply wearing her life away, draining her entire nerve force

on mere household drudgery. The husbands of those women would
be overcome with self-contempt if it were necessary for their wives
to go out and earn a living—*to earn a living*, at least there would be
some *living*, to it, not the slow, miserable death-in-life that I see go
on about me."

Lotus was left with many thoughts that night, but there was
a reigning thought, a sweet consciousness that kept the tender smile
twinkling at the corners of her lips.

Lotus smiled sweetly in her dreams; she was very young, and
to her many of the trials of woman's lot were beyond the power of
imagination. She was sure she loved wisely; the man of her dreams
was the man with whom she had worked almost daily for two
years. She knew him, and he knew her. There had never passed
words of love between them, but Lotus felt a sweet security in his
quiet affection for her. Did he not always bring her his letters from
home, read to her messages from his mother, tell her of his home in
dear old Frankfort? Was it not to her that he always brought tickets
for the latest concert, or some particularly interesting lecture?
Did he not always think of her, was he not always constant in his
attentions?

She had heard that women did make mistakes and give their
hearts to men that were unsympathetic, but surely their married life
would be ideal. They had the same tastes, the same hopes. Professor
Schurer was a man that would be proud of his wife's success and
would watch her work with real deep interest, and she, on her part,
would be equally interested in his. It would a marriage of soul, of
mind, and heart. No wonder Lotus was happy.

XI

It was some time after this that Helen began to notice a great change in Lotus. Day by day she grew thin and pale, and her usual energy and child-like enthusiasm were fast disappearing, Helen well knew the cause of Lotus's unhappiness. She had watched Professor Schurer closely and long ago she had become convinced that his friendship for Lotus would never grow into a warmer sentiment. Helen's judgment was keen; she knew men, and further she knew German men, and knew their ideas of marital felicity. A true German would never imagine that a student such as Lotus, a woman who devoted herself to chemical research, whose aim was to teach that beloved science, could possess the requisite qualities of a wife. Helen had much behind her in the past that taught her to read men's hearts. Women's hearts, read rightly, often serve to interpret the actions of the opposite sex.

Helen struggled alone with her anxiety. It was a heavy burden upon Helen, for she loved Lotus with a passionate love; all her hopes, all her own womanly longings had been turned into the channel of Lotus's future. In her unhappiness she lived again her own bitter trial. One day, in conversation with her friend Kate Dunning, the secret came out and Helen opened her heart to the one woman whose completely happy life she envied.

The Dunnings were a marvelous couple, who actually lived as others always said they were going to live some day. They were not well-to-do people, and so, instead of cramping themselves in some Harlem flat, or boarding in two rooms in some fashionable neighborhood, they had the courage and faith in themselves to rent a small home with a big piazza and some grounds in Fort Washington.

The Dunnings did not share the prevailing theories of the division of duties in the family. Mr. Dunning conducted his business down town, and Mrs. Dunning conducted hers up town. To Kate Dunning the care of the house was not the crowning glory of wifehood. Neither did she believe that man must necessarily make the money, and woman absorb herself merely in spending it. A life without some earnest occupation would have been dreary and empty to her. And so her little Kindergarten, which she had organized some years before, was not given up, but merely moved to the "country," as most people insisted in calling Fort Washington, in total disregard of the map of the metropolis.

Kate's Kindergarten had been a great success, and now, eight years after her marriage, its most hopeful pupil was her own, bright, winning boy. Yes, unheard-of as it may seem, Kate Dunning was a mother and a *Kindergärtnerin*, and her friends can vouch for it that her home was always comfortable and that the internal machinery (or infernal machinery, as some have cause enough to say) worked smoothly and noiselessly.

I think—and Helen thought—John Dunning was a hero. At first, in the early days of his marriage, many poked fun at him for letting his wife earn her living instead of his doing it for her. It was noticeable, however, that none ever teased twice. Not that he was ill-tempered, but convincing. Old Mrs. Dunning had been greatly shocked—"What, her son not able to support his wife decently?"— John had had a quiet talk with his mother which silenced her, even if it failed to win her. It at least convinced her that there no interference would be permitted.

"My dear mother," he had said, "it simply means that I prefer to engage my wife as a *Kindergärtnerin*, while others prefer theirs to be cooks or seamstresses."

Mrs. Dunning thought her John was slightly demented, but he continued, "Why should I insist upon Kate's being cooped up in a room, washing dishes, cutting out dresses, darning socks, rolling piecrust, or cleaning bric-a-brac, when she can earn enough at her Kindergarten to pay for a good cook and a competent chambermaid and seamstress? You know if I forced her to give up her Kindergarten, it would force her to give up many of the pleasantest features about our home. From a satisfied, active, sympathetic companion as she has always been, bless her! she would soon degenerate into one of those nervous, discontented, narrow-minded, and unsympathetic wives that men often force their better halves into becoming. I declare it's more than I can understand, how men can willfully cramp the souls of their life companions into the mental horizon of a maid of all work."

Again I say John Dunning was a hero, and many were the quiet battles fought. What sympathy he met with when it leaked out that his wife never held a needle in her hand from January till June. But John smiled and said;

"I am not ashamed to say, our Maria darns my socks better than her mistress could, but," he added, with his face aglow, "there are many things which Kate can do that Maria is not quite so handy at."

People watched John, in the sly hope of noting a neglected tear, a missing button, or a frayed elbow, but John was too clever for them. He knew a frayed elbow on him meant an endless amount of gossip over his wife, and so rigorously watched himself, and unmanlike actually brought his own clothes himself to be repaired. He even critically eyed his own cravats, and endeavored not to forget to brush his hat. Kate thought his care of his own appearance was one of the sweetest tributes he paid her; she knew what it meant, and what a bore it must be to him.

And when the baby came! No one dreamed of the quiet happiness that was Kate's. How could the world imagine that a woman that didn't make a bit of the outfit herself, that didn't even approve of feather-stitching on flannel skirts, could possibly take any pride in her baby! And Kate stolidly refused to acknowledge that machine-made clothes were necessarily any less comfortable and wholesome than clothes that had taken hours and hours of wearisome stitching and broken backs and weak eyes "because baby's things must all be hand-made." Of course people generally conceded that Kate Dunning's child would look like a little orphan, and that was the end of it. Strange to say, I think, Baby Dunning inherited some of his father's resolution and pride, for he seemed to understand that it was incumbent upon him to look clean and neat whenever mamma's friends aimed their critical eyes upon him. They never found his bibs soiled nor his frock torn, nor his toes coming through his socks; in fact none of their dismal prophecies came true. And how can we account for it that a healthy, lively boy could always seem to be clean and neat unless he was actuated by the brave determination in his little breast not to give satisfaction to the army of critics which was solemnly arrayed against his own dear mamma?

XII

Helen promised herself a rare treat, and had visited her friends,
the Dunnings, one Sunday at their charming home overlooking
the Hudson. It was late October, there had been some very sudden
changes of temperature, and never before did the shores bear such
a glorious wealth of color. Glancing out of the library window, and
seeing the bright blue water below with a white yacht or two on it,
the wall of deep red and yellow foliage beyond, and the soft clear
sky above, Helen sighed heavily.

"Oh, what perfect peace and quiet this is; what a change,
what a divine sense of rest comes over one here after the
cobblestones of New York. Do you know, when I get here a
shame comes over me, a very shame for the crazy, unnatural life
I lead. There, just look out at that picture; see that long line of
majestic, hospitable elms, see that winding soft brown road, and
just look at that single birch gleaming so pure and white. And do
you know, I have the strangest fancy, I actually prefer the winter
landscape to the spring. To most people there is a sadness about
bare trees, but to me there is nothing more exquisitely beautiful
than the delicate etchings of those fine, graceful, slender limbs
against the sky."

"Yes, it is a beautiful picture," said Kate, with her arms about
Helen's waist. "I confess I am very happy here. And yet," she said
suddenly, with a light laugh, "only yesterday, one of your city folks
condoled with me, saying 'It must be so trying out there in the
wilderness; whatever do you find to do with yourself any way?'"

69

Helen smiled: "And I am willing to guess you answered mildly and sweetly; I should have been cross and impolite—I know I should. That sort of patronizing of one's dearest hopes and aims, which is encountered in society, goads me fearfully."

At that moment Kate's husband entered the room with his bright curly-haired boy. They were dressed for a tramp. Kate kissed them good-by, and then turned to Helen:

"My dear," she said, "when one has all this, how can one mind such trifles?"

There were tears in Helen's eyes, "O Kate," she exclaimed, "and I am growing more and more bitter every day. It seems to me as if the world always turns its wrong side to me."

"Now, Helen," replied her friend gently, "this won't do, you are overtired. Come up here with Lotus, and have a few days' rest. I've noticed Lotus is looking a little pale lately. We'll have to give her some country air, too."

Helen sank into a chair, "Poor Lotus," she said. "And have you noticed it?"

"Why, Helen, what is the matter? Is she ill?"

Helen pressed Kate's hand, "Perhaps I ought to tell you. It is killing me, keeping it all to myself and brooding over it."

"Helen, you frighten me. I thought Lotus was so happy, and I thought you were so contented that she cared for Professor Schurer. Now, what has taken place, doesn't she care for him?"

"Anyone could see that. O Kate, that is not the trouble."

"But he's been so attentive, and he took her to that entire Fiske course, and he never goes to a concert that he doesn't ask her to go with him, and their work in the laboratory brings them together so sweetly. I think it's the most perfect match I've ever seen."

Helen laid her hand on Kate's shoulder, "If it weren't for you and your blessed John, my faith in double blessedness would be gone."

Why, how can you—there, stop your work; you are growing desperately morbid, take a vacation."

"I am growing cynical, but how can one help it? Here I've watched Professor Schurer and Lotus and have longed to see them married, watching with fond and foolish eyes how suited they were to one another. Kate, if you select a man and a woman who seem to be made for each other, be sure that one or the other—generally the man—will love some third person. It doesn't seem to be the law of love to *suit one another*. How can one understand it? I am perfectly positive that Professor Schurer admires Lotus greatly, I think he esteems her above any other woman, he likes her grit, thinks she is going to make her mark. He loves her sweet disposition, he basks in her genial ways, he looks anxious when she is overworked, and—"

"And?"

"And he's no more in love with her than he is with you or me."

"Oh, you don't tell me!"

"There I see him, day by day, growing deeper and deeper in love with that little numskull of a Brown girl."

"What? Maria Brown's daughter? Just because he boards there!"

"Don't ask me; I'm too much exasperated. Can you tell me what there is in that girl?"

"Blue eyes, and beautiful auburn hair."

"Exactly. Now, that's what makes me lose faith in man and in the future."

"But, Helen, this is an old story, that men will marry for passion, and not true esteem and affection."

"True; an old story. But it was not so bad fifty years ago. A woman did not look for anything else. She was more ready to marry the man that was attracted to her, and did not demand so much."

"That's true."

"Now women have professions, interests, and opinions of their own. They look for sympathy; they must have it. No longer can they absorb themselves entirely in being household utilities and domestic animals. But, tell me, how are they going to get sympathy, how are they going to get husbands that will respect their individuality, when the only men that are capable of understanding, of appreciating such women—men like Johann Schurer—go off and marry their Molly Browns? What will be the end of it all?"

"But, Helen," mildly interposed Kate, "my dear girl, you are talking of men only. Do not women as well lose their hearts to utterly unworthy men?"

Helen drew a deep breath, and looked away for a moment. "I say no; women are not so apt to stoop to inferior men; or, if one is in love with an unsympathetic man, she often controls her feelings. But that is not the question—pardon me, it is not. The question is: Why are the women that do commit such a mistake always unhappy, and why are the men never so? You cannot tell me that a woman can be happy who does not find sympathy and congeniality in her home, whose higher instincts and noblest aims are kept secreted from her husband. But the magnificent men that are happy with their Molly Browns are legion. There are any number of men that, as the husbands of their Mollies, apparently do not find anything is lacking. It is so easy for them to go elsewhere for their intellectual stimulus."

"Why, Helen, how you go on!"

"Yes, for I am wound up now, and I shall not stop yet. It's in me; I've been smothering it for so long."

"Go on, my dear; you'll feel better when it's out of you."

"It's no joking matter. Here is one of the greatest problems for the future to solve. How can the woman of the future be happily married? or is she to renounce it forever? Is the highest type of woman destined never to be handed down to the succeeding generation? Is the noblest work of woman to be left in the hands of the lowest of her sex? I have seen an editorial in a prominent woman's journal lately, which seemed to think the problem would be solved if professional women would not marry. It seemed to think that a certain number of women as well as a certain number of men never marry. Let those women, it said, that care to absorb themselves and lose their identity marry if they wish; but let this idea that all women should marry, that wifehood and motherhood are the crowning glories of a woman's lot, die a natural death. I have noticed a hostile attitude toward marriage among a great many of our most intellectual women, and I am very sorry to see it. I think it is very unfortunate. The problem of marriage will never be solved by *Punch's* immortal 'Don't.' Can any true woman acknowledge that to be the solution of it? Is it wise for women simply to give up the struggle, and turn their backs on marriage, saying, 'Such is not for us?' Either one of two things must come to pass. It seems to me, either men must become dissatisfied with physical marriages, and must look for intellectual and spiritual marriage as well; or, if women do marry their inferiors, they will have to assume the same liberty that the married man possesses to-day."

"Why, what can you mean? Not the same moral standards, I hope."

"Oh, no; but if women are doomed to uncongenial wedded life then they must learn not to look for too much from it—they must learn, like the men, to take love—marriage—parenthood *en passant* not to make it the business of life."

"Surely you would not approve of that!"

"Surely not! The only real way to the ideal marriage is the demand on the part of men for more than physical satisfaction. I refer to the demand for housekeepers and cooks when I say this, quite as much as another kind of physical satisfaction—it all answers physical needs. Marriage becomes purified and ennobled just so far as the higher claims of soul and mind enter into it. Thus far marriage has been governed by the spirit of man; little by little the finer, more delicate claims of woman are being respected. A great work on the History of Human Marriage closes with the inspiring words: 'The History of Human Marriage is the history of a relation in which women have been gradually triumphing over the passions, the prejudices, and the selfish interests of men.' But there is a great deal still to be accomplished. It is a vexed problem and will be for some time to come."

XIII

Louise Skidmore sat down and fairly cried with vexation. This was
the second affair that week she had been obliged to forego, because
at the last moment her husband had been unable to accompany
her.

"Now, my darling, you know it isn't my fault, you know
I would much rather go with you than have to take that long,
tiresome trip to Washington. I am very sorry, but can't you send for
your brother?"

"You know Fred is at Tuxedo."

"Can't you send for the Manns? They'll take you."

"No; Cecily is going to dine first with the Marshes, and then
they were to go together."

Harold paced up and down impatiently. The coupé stood at
the door, his satchels were in the hall, it was time to leave. It was
unfortunate to have a wife that minds your leaving town suddenly.
Was it possible for him to put off an important piece of business at
the White House in order to escort his wife to a ball?

"My dear little woman, now do cheer up. You know you are
proud that your husband is wanted all over at the same moment,
you have told me so yourself. Do take courage, and be a brave little
woman. If you are nervous send for someone to stay with you, I'll
be back in a day or two, probably by to-morrow evening."

"Good-by, I'm all right. Hurry up now, or you'll miss the
train." But a sudden glance at the lovely new costume lying on the
bed brought the tears back, and Harold left the house sorry for

his wife indeed, but feeling rather sore that she should take it so to heart, and act as if he were really neglecting her, when he was obliged to go off on business. It wasn't his fault; did he go for fun? Didn't he have the hardest part of it? At least she had a comfortable bed to sleep in, while he would be tossing to and fro on his berth, rattling along to Washington. It seemed to him as if she ought to have something more substantial to amuse her than a ball or a theater party. He smiled to himself as he thought how he would enjoy one quiet evening to himself. How he would relish sitting night after night in a snug library surrounded with all his favorites. Oh, that would be happiness! And Louise, who had all the time she wanted, he doubted if it ever occurred to her to sit there for a moment. If she ever did any reading, it was a light novel, generally French, and she preferred to stretch herself cozily upon her boudoir lounge and munch *bon-bons* while she read.

Well, he had chosen this beautiful, indolent, spoilt woman for his wife. He admired her; he loved her passionately. She answered perfectly to certain moods of his; she was always dressed in perfect taste, she presided over their home with a delightful charm; when he was out with her he felt proud of her, she was so beautiful, so graceful, so bewitching. He was not jealous of all the attention that was showered upon her and was glad to find she was amused by it. He often felt that he could not offer her sufficient amusement himself and he was glad that others could offer it. He loved his wife a great deal, but he kept only one side of his life for her. She was his Priestess of the Beautiful; his Goddess of Ease and Luxury; he never thought of asking her to share his worries, and he never felt the necessity for doing so. Why cause a line to destroy the beauty of that smooth, white brow? And he imagined that he preferred it so. Thus he could come home and forget all his cares;

his home was a place whence disagreeable thoughts were to be rigorously banished.

There was no doubt but that sometimes, rarely, Harold did turn to the past with just the ghost of a pang. He felt that a marriage with Helen would have been more completely rounded; that there would have been less regret on his part, for instance, when obliged to leave his wife for a business trip. He could not help but smile as he thought of Helen being ennuied by having to remain alone. He pictured her seated in the library enjoying some book that they would be sure to talk over together the next day, but then there was the disagreeable and equally lifelike picture of Helen being left at home and putting on her bonnet to attend some meeting or some consultation, or to perform some dreadful operation, and coming home to him smelling of ether and iodoform and such abominations. And the time might have come when Harold had no engagements, when he had come home free for once and happy in the expectation of a quiet evening spent together, like as not, just that evening Helen would have some important work to do, work that could not be put off. How uncomfortable to have a wife whose duties would interfere with the comfort, with the social life of a home. Why, what man would bear it? To the woman the home should come above all things. It was obviously her duty to be the center of the home life.

Still sometimes, only sometimes, Harold could not refrain from wishing that women like Helen had something of the Louise about them, or that the Louises had more of the Helen in them. The line between such women was too sharply drawn for comfort. Why were women either dolls or steam engines?

XIV

Dr. Brent's office hours were just over. With a sigh of relief she leaned back in her comfortable chair, with her feet crossed on the hearth. She was glad that the day's work was done. She had been fretted more than usual to-day. One particular incident had annoyed and worried her, even more than she had liked to admit to herself. One of her patients had remarked:

"I see Mr. Skidmore has accepted the Presidency of the Municipal Health League."

This was no surprise to Helen, since she had been Chairman of the Nominating Committee. Harold and she often met at public meetings, for each played an important part in the philanthropic movements of the day.

"There are some more duties for him," added the lady bitingly, "I don't see how his wife stands it. I for one don't blame her one bit, no I don't."

"Blame her," thought Helen. "Now I wonder what on earth she can mean?" But she answered coldly, "I suppose Mrs. Skidmore is as proud of her husband as we all are of him." Her patient laughed lightly.

"Oh, yes; of course, certainly. Very proud of him, but it seems to me that's hardly enough for a wife, is it? You want to know something more of your husband than his picture in the daily papers, don't you?"

"Why, surely, Mrs. Blagden—" protested Helen.

"Oh, come, now don't go off into one of your indignation spells," she exclaimed. "Of course, he doesn't positively neglect his wife; you don't think a Skidmore would do that! Hasn't she the handsomest rubies this season, and aren't her teas the most uncomfortably crowded in all New York? And hasn't she plenty of gallant cavaliers? At least she is sure of one who is a host in himself."

Then Helen had stopped her and had left the house, but she could not wave those idle words away from her all day. What did it mean? Could it be that Harold could neglect his wife, neglect her so as to make it common talk? It was not like Harold, and yet, she could not help think uncomfortably of how busy he was, and how impossible it must be for him to see very much of her, and was she strong enough to stand alone? Had she any resources of her own against ennui, loneliness? Helen could not help remember Harold's words to her when he left her, saying she would never be able to reconcile the duties of marriage with her ambitions. Was he making the same mistake? And what *did* that woman mean to insinuate?"

But tired and perplexed as she was, her eyes were bright with expectation, for to-night she was to hear her favorite opera, "Götterdämmerung," which she had not heard since her student days in Germany. A few days before she had confessed to one of her patients that she had never heard "Götterdämmerung" in America, and she was persuaded to accompany her in the family box. There was no escape, although Helen would have greatly preferred sitting alone in some quiet corner of the dress circle where she could listen unobserved.

When Helen entered the box, she was its only occupant, although the overture was just about to begin. The rows of empty boxes frowned at her depressingly. Here and there was a solitary

occupant like herself, someone equally unversed in the manners
of good society. The overture began, and Helen wondered how
all these people could afford to miss it. What an opera it is. The
passionate rhapsody of *Brünnhilde's* parting with *Siegfried* shook
Helen's soul. What had *Brünnhilde* not given up? Immortality,
Godhead, her wild, free, natural existence, rushing along with the
force of the clouds, flying before the winds of the Heavens; all,
all this for the love of a man, for the love of a man who would
soon forget her love, forget it for a simple maiden, who was
but a star next to *Brünnhilde's* glorious sun-light. And how with
this Renunciation, this past behind her, could she yet sing so
rapturously, so gloriously of love, of true womanhood?

Ah, was there not reason why this music, this apotheosis
of passion, should shake Helen from her very soul? The story of
Brünnhilde was the old Saga, old, very old, but is not the same
story enacted to-day, only the tale is somewhat changed? *Wotan*—
public opinion—says to *Brünnhilde*—the woman that has dared
to step out of the usual course of dependence and uselessness—
So thou hast defied me, the God of the world. Thou hast taken
thy charger and hast sped on to tracks that have been forbidden
thee. Thou hast willfully separated thyself from thy sisters, who
obediently follow where I lead. And for this sin thou shalt be cut
off from the natural sphere of thy womanhood. For this shall the
great and all-powerful *Wotan* teach thee that he shall not be defied.
For this shall *Wotan* doom thee to He throughout the ages as if
dead, but verily sleeping, surrounded by mountains of ice and frost.
The gleam of the sun upon the glaciers shall cause many to draw
nigh attracted, but when they see the mountains upon mountains
of ice that have to be scaled, the icy breath of the frost to be passed
through, they will be daunted and a great fear shall be upon them

and they shall flee. And behold not until thy hero Cometh—not until thy *Siegfried* shall appear, shalt thou be released from thy deep sleep, which is as death. When thy hero cometh, thy *Siegfried*, then shall the mountains of ice and the thick walls of the glaciers melt away and disappear, even as ice melts before the flame."

This is the modern Saga of *Brünnhilde* but it is far more tragic than the Saga of yore. The *Siegfried* that shall come dauntless to face the ice and frost will have to be a greater hero than even *Siegfried*, the hero of old. For many a man is led on by the glare of passion, by the flaming breath of love, and who wouldn't turn back from them fearing to be scorched? When higher and higher leap the flames about *Brünnhilde's* couch—higher and higher mount the answering flames in her lover's heart. But the impetuous lover's breast to be chilled by the icy frost, the intrepid voyager to proceed on when his passion congeals within him in the frigid air that sweeps over from the mountains of ice! Oh, a great, a bold, a valiant *Siegfried* does it take to pierce below all this and reach the warm glow, the fierce fire that is steadily burning beneath this ice and frost! A fire that will rise and leap up, up, up, when the surrounding frost melts away and the great heart of flame is laid bare.... "Oh, there she is, prompt, of course. My dear Dr. Brent, you must excuse us; let me present my little cousin. Miss Daisy Cuttle, one of our *débutantes*, you know, from Cayuga. We had such a horribly long dinner, I thought we should never get here, but then we've heard the 'Götterdämmerung' so often."

Helen shivered; the upturned faces of the audience went through her inexperienced soul like a knife. A low murmur of reproach finally silenced the speaker, and Helen vainly endeavored to again concentrate her attention upon the opera. Notwithstanding the fact that her patient was one of the most fashionable leaders in New York, and that the box she was in was the most richly appointed in the opera house, Helen did not feel proud of her surroundings; again and again she regretted that she had been persuaded to accept the invitation. We have seen before that Helen had very wrong notions of many things, and we know her bump of social reverence was either totally missing, or at least very strangely placed, quite in the wrong spot, for she certainly reverenced things that it was obviously absurd to reverence.

Just think of the difficulty of the task before me to awaken any sympathy or interest for a heroine that not only does not feel herself honored by reposing in the finest satin-cushioned chairs in the opera house, but that if asked would not have been aware that she was with the very best society of the entire audience. A heroine that would have pointed (I am almost afraid to acknowledge it) to the dress circle, and maybe a little higher up, if asked to point out the best society in the place?

In fact, quite a strange little incident took place during the performance of another opera that same season, when she had found herself in the balcony next to a small nervous woman, who evidently wanted to get the very most of her night's treat. This woman, not dreaming that the quietly dressed woman next to her could have anything to do with all those fine people in the boxes, remarked with a sigh that she wished she could know who all the great folks were. Her neighbor leaned over:

"I think I can tell you, madam." The little woman looked pleased, and Helen continued, obeying a sudden impulse, You wish to know who are all the best people here, do you not? You want me to point out the very best society?" The little woman was delighted.

"Look up there in the gallery, way up there in the corner. Do you see that pale woman who is leaning over very much absorbed during the last act—perhaps you noticed that she carried a very heavy book? That is the score of the opera, and she follows every note of it eagerly. She is a poor music teacher, who supports a widowed mother and a crippled sister. She has saved for many a day to hear this opera, and even then would not have used the money had not her mother with tears in her eyes beseeched her to go." The little woman on her left had never turned her eyes *upward*, and so she admitted.

"Then you see that poor, little sickly, deformed boy with the big head up there on the last row? He is a genius; some day I hope to get our wealthy people interested in him. If he can have a fine education, he will be one of our great musicians." The little woman grew impatient.

"But," she said, "I wanted to know those great folks down in the boxes, those that have on so many diamonds, and such fine dresses, and the big bouquets; I would like to know if they are the folks I've read so much about in the papers. I know some of their names, but I don't know them all. Here is a list of them," she said, holding up her programme. "It's been some help to me, but I can't quite make it all out. But," she said, turning away with a sigh, "I suppose the likes of you and me don't know them. They ain't for us." Her neighbor turned to her again.

"Pardon me," she said. "I think you asked me to point out to you the best society here, the best people—in fact, 'the great folks,' I think you said. I have done so. I mean it seriously."

The little woman's eyes grew big, "Now you're chaffing me," she said. I don't know that her ideas of social economics were any changed by this chance conversation.

But I have been guilty of a great digression. Well, on this particular night the usual chatter went on about Helen. There was little Miss Daisy, the *débutantes*, who, one might have thought, would be delighted with the music, at least during her first season, and would have listened. But no, she must imitate her elders, and her little white shoulders, of which too much entirely might be seen, went bobbing up and down, and the little red lips went buzz, buzz, buzz, quite like the more hardened sinners. The looks of annoyance aimed at them from below—looks that went through Helen and made her tingle with mortification—created absolutely no impression whatever upon little Miss Daisy, who smiled amiably, and who seemed to regard herself as particularly distinguished. Now Helen happened to know Miss Daisy's parents—good, honest, country people, who were distantly related to Mrs. Crane, and who thought it would be just the greatest thing in the world for their daughter if she would be taken under her wing and given the polish of a winter or two in New York's best society. Helen was positive they had no idea of the kind of costume Daisy was sporting in that best society, had no idea that Miss Daisy's chaperon had insisted on buying an entirely new outfit for the simple little country girl. Helen could hear Miss Daisy saying:

"Isn't that Mrs. Keith-Brew—Oh, there's Charlie Borne again, in the Marsh box. I guess they've engaged. Look what gorgeous flowers Mamie Marsh has." And this to the accompaniment of the most sublime music that ever greeted mortal ears!

At last came the *entr'acte* when talking was at least legitimized. A large number of young men danced in and out of the box, as Miss Daisy was already a great favorite, and there was the additional attraction, for more highly seasoned tastes, of Mrs. Belmar, the handsome and gay widow, who was always overflowing with spicy news and witty take-offs of her friends. She was all white skin, black eyes, black tulle, and diamonds. Dr. Brent moved restlessly about in her chair. The conversation going on about her was hardly calculated to either stimulate or interest her.

Miss Daisy—white lace and pearls:

"Isn't Wagner dull?"

Male voice number one: "Yes; it would have been insufferable if my box hadn't been immediately opposite yours."

Black tulle and diamonds—suppressing a yawn:

"Do tell us something exciting, can't you? I've done my, very best to stay awake."

White lace and pearls: "Oh, good-evening, Mr. Price; are you an ardent admirer of Wagner?"

Male voice number two: "Well, to tell the truth, I don't know Wagner from Bellini; I never did. But Richard's all the rage, so of course I fall dutifully into line." Loud laughter.

Black tulle and diamonds: "Behave yourself; how dreadful! aren't you ashamed of yourself, sir?"

Mrs. Crane—red velvet and rubies: "I don't believe it; Louise Skidmore is a beautiful little goose, but she's no worse than that." Helen listened with a beating heart.

Black tulle and diamonds: "To be stupid is the worst crime of all, in society. Just watch them for a minute; here, take my glasses and see how her diamond necklace goes pit-a-pat, pit-a-pat, and just watch his eyes; he positively can't take them off of her. Why, the pair are making a perfect exhibition of themselves!"

White lace and pearls: "But isn't he divinely handsome?"

Male voice number two: "Where is Mr. Skidmore?"

Red velvet and rubies (dryly): "Mr. Skidmore has no time for the opera."

Black tulle and diamonds: "No, nor for his wife either."

Red velvet and rubies: "Then, where's the harm in poor Louise having an escort? She can't stay at home and mope all night, can she?"

Male voice number two: "Ha, ha, ha! No harm in the least, not the slightest, not the least in the world."

Chorus: "Ha, ha, ha!" All seemed to enjoy the excellent joke.

Helen raised her glasses, and looked across at the Skidmore box. She saw Mrs. Skidmore, looking radiantly beautiful. She wore a corsage wonderfully and fearfully made. It seemed to be entirely of feathers of a blue-black tinge, and the light falling on them made them seem almost alive; it was cut very low, and the beautiful white neck arched exquisitely up to the soft auburn hair. There was a deep flush on her cheeks, as if she were conscious of the dozens of opera glasses aimed at her from all parts of the house. Slightly behind her, toying with her magnificent feather fan, and gazing very speakingly at her was Mortimer Stuart Verplanck.

Helen dropped her glasses with a little shiver. She leaned back in her chair; she felt the blood rush from her face.

"Why, my dear doctor, aren't you well? you are as pale as a ghost."

"Why, doctor, you must take my vinaigrette."

"Doctor, this won't do. We shall have to prescribe for you."

At last, at last, the opera was over. Fancy being glad, relieved that the "Götterdämmerung" was over. But the place had become almost unendurable to her since she had seen those two in the box opposite to her. God! Was that man to enter her life again? Was he to cut down another flower? Was he still at large, feeding upon the purity, the innocence of the most beautiful, the most lovable women of society? Where was conscience, where was decency? She had no doubt that had Mortimer Stuart Verplanck entered the box. Miss Daisy would have been all smiles, and she would have edged that he might take the seat next to her. Doubtless she had already been instructed that Mortimer Stuart Verplanck, although a widower, was considered the best catch in town, altogether the best family in New York to marry into. "And Harold, Harold," groaned Helen, "who is it now that is casting off all that is sweet in life, all that is dearest, for ambition, for worldly success, for fame?"

XV

As Harold sat in his office, surrounded by a thousand papers, and endeavoring to put his mind upon them, he was in reality thinking of his wife. He was not at all satisfied with her condition. It was all very well to be told that it was natural, that after the birth of her child she would regain her normal condition, etc., etc. But still he was not easy. It was not pleasant to see his beautiful, self-possessed Louise reduced to a state of nervousness and lassitude from which it seemed impossible to arouse her. It was not pleasant to have her burst into tears almost at any glance that was cast upon her. It was not pleasant to have her shrink from his touch as if she were afraid of him. There was no use, he could not put his mind upon his business, and so he resolved to call upon Dr. Manning and have a little quiet talk with him. Dr. Manning welcomed him cordially. He smiled at Harold's fears.

"A mere nothing, my dear sir, a mere nothing. It will all pass away. Merely a bit nervous. Natural enough, in her condition, you know; a little hyperaesthetic, that is all. Pull yourself together. You had better be taking a tonic, and you will see all these fears will come to nothing. In a time like this, my dear sir, all we need is a little patience—a little patience, my dear Mr. Skidmore, and we shall see everything the same as before."

Harold was forced to rest satisfied, and to possess his soul with patience. Nevertheless, he was uneasy. It was difficult, with all his faith in Dr. Manning, to attribute all Louise's eccentricities to this state of hyper-something.

Meanwhile the doctors handsome brougham stood at the door for many hours. A consultation was had with two of the greatest authorities, but nothing was decided but to await coming events with as much equanimity as possible.

One day Harold came into his wife's room to take leave before going to his office. She smiled faintly as he entered.

"I want to ask you a favor."

"What is it? You know, dear, I shall grant it if it be in my power."

"I know it: let me see Dr. Brent." Harold started back in dismay.

"Dr. Brent?" he repeated vaguely.

"I know it seems foolish, but I have an idea that if I have her I shall get well. But you mustn't tell Dr. Manning; I think he would be mad. Promise you will get Dr. Brent to come in, but don't tell Dr. Manning."

"But what foolish idea is this? What does it mean?"

"Oh, I know you don't approve of women doctors, but let me try just this once; I have heard of her doing such wonderful things. Do let me have her, Harold."

"It isn't that I disapprove of women doctors; send for anyone you want."

"Then you will let me have her?"

"No, no; anyone you want but her," added Harold hastily. "There are a great many others."

"But you know there isn't one with her reputation. Why, what makes you so set against poor Dr. Brent?" Harold could only murmur:

"No, it is impossible. Ask anything else but that." He left the room abruptly. As he closed the door he thought he heard the words, "I shall die, I shall die."

All the morning these half-whispered words of his wife rang in his ears. He could think of nothing else. To be sure it had at first struck him as impossible that Helen should treat his wife. Still, there was really no harm in it, and on thinking over the idea, some of the incongruity disappeared. Besides, he could not stand those words of his wife. So he looked up Helen's office in the directory and, jumping into a cab, was soon at her door.

It was office hours, and he was obliged to wait in the waiting room. He looked about him. He was the only gentleman among half a dozen ladies. A neat little buttons had ushered him in promptly, and he found himself in the most attractive waiting room he had ever seen. There was a great deal of soft warm color about the room. There was no carpet; the floor was a bright polished wood, but it was covered profusely with richly tinted rugs of those beautiful, dull Oriental tones. The sofas and chairs were neat and comfortable, some rich maroon, and others dull Persian blue. Several small oak tables were covered with the latest magazines, and on the walls, which were painted a delicate green, were many fine etchings.

As he sat waiting, he took up one of the magazines and carelessly turned its pages. He saw an article, on the "Public Kindergarten System," by Helen Brent, M.D. On the cover of the magazine was a special announcement of her article, which was evidently considered the chief card of the month. He could not help but think what a complete, full, rich life was Helen's. Looking about the room, he was sure the ladies were among the most exclusive circles in the city. Two or three faces were familiar to him. He smiled with a sort of deprecatory shame at the thought that he had once dared to persuade this woman to leave her work, to give up her profession, her life work, and accept him in their stead.

Hearing the office door open he stepped out into the hall to say he only wished to speak to the doctor a moment, and to ask if he could be permitted to enter without delay. Harold was surprised to see that Helen was not very calm, although it was evident that she was making a strong effort at self-control. He noticed with pity that she looked very tired. There were dull shadows under her eyes, and her skin was not as smooth and clear as it used to be. They shook hands formally.

"I am afraid you work too hard," he said. She shook her head and motioned him to a seat. "Doctor," he continued, "I have a coupé outside; it will wait until you are disengaged. My wife is very ill, I am afraid; she has asked for you; I beg that you will come as soon as possible."

"Yes," she said quietly. "Who has been in attendance?"

"Dr. Manning," answered Harold impatiently, as if he could not see what connection that had with the case.

"Does he know you've called upon me?"

Harold told Helen of his wife's whim that he should not be informed. Helen smiled.

"But I cannot visit Dr. Manning's patient," she said. Harold made a gesture of impatience.

"I cannot see—" he began; Helen interrupted him.

"I shall be happy to see your wife in consultation with Dr. Manning."

"But we are losing valuable time, and she has set her heart upon Dr. Manning not knowing a word of your coming."

"But I could not consent to that, and it would not be for the patient's good that I should." Harold murmured something about "women's nonsense," but Helen replied coldly:

"Pardon me, but you do not understand. This is no woman's foolish whim. I am acting no differently from any one of my colleagues. You doubtless think I am not bound by the usual etiquette of the profession—what does a woman doctor care about those things? On the contrary, I am a regular member of the County Medical Society and of the Academy, and I am judged no differently from the other members. I shall be at your service all the afternoon. If you will kindly send me word when Dr. Manning will be able to meet me, I shall be happy to call and see your wife with him; or, at least, I must have his permission to see her alone."

Harold rose. "Good-day," he said.

"Good-day, Mr. Skidmore."

XVI

Harold laid his quandary before Dr. Manning, who courteously arranged that Mrs, Skidmore should be humored. Accordingly Dr. Manning and Dr. Brent talked the case over, and it was given into Dr. Brent's hands.

Helen had many incentives to do her utmost. Chief among the varying motives was the hope that Mrs. Skidmore, once restored to health, might again become united with her husband and throw aside past influences. Helen had strong hopes that she might succeed in awakening Harold to a proper sense of the responsibilities of married life. She saw in Louise a beautiful, vain, weak woman; a woman that needed an atmosphere of luxury and adulation; a woman above all that needed to lean on some stronger character. This stronger character she should have had in her husband, but Helen, and indeed all the world, knew that the active public life of the Honorable Harold Skidmore left but little room for the fulfillment of any demands that married life might make of him.

So far as Helen could see, Harold's life ran upon precisely the same lines after his marriage to the beautiful Miss Gushing of Baltimore as during his bachelorhood. Indeed, since that time, each year saw him more prominent in his profession, more active in reforms, and more in demand for all sorts of public meetings, from an after-dinner speech to presiding at the latest Indignation Meeting, receiving at the Club's reception, or introducing the latest distinguished foreigner on the occasion of his opening lecture. New

York, indeed the whole country, needed him, and all voted that there was but one Harold Skidmore, and that no one could take his place.

Now, in the face of all this could anyone blame him that he neglected to accompany his wife to the opera, or sometimes failed to preside over the distribution of the joint at his own table; who could be so narrow as to claim that for such a man the duties to his fellow-countrymen do not come first? Did you say, "Then such a man ought not to marry?" Pshaw, my dear friend, you are Puritanical, absurd! Why, if the world were to agree with you, where would be our college presidents, our statesmen, our ministers, our doctors, our lawyers? All within the pale of dismal bachelordom? You see to what your fanatical ideas would bring you.

I hear you whispering something about women, how the world judges them; I do not quite grasp what you mean; you know your position is untenable, so you are afraid to speak above your breath. Do you ask, "Why is it that professional women dare not marry unless they are prepared to reshape their lives on new lines? Why does the world poke and pry into the married lives of such women to see if John goes without warm mufflers, or if his socks go darnless, or if the bread is doughy, when it concerns itself only with one side of the great question?" Ah, well, why discuss it further? It was a problem constantly in Helen's mind, but she found very few that cared to discuss it with her. People opened wide their eyes, refused to see the analogy, fell back on the original axioms upon the ways of the world—such is life—what are you going to do about it?—you can't change human nature, etc., etc.

But there was not much room in Helen's busy life just now to be pondering over problems. There was work to do, hard work, and she bent all her forces to it.

Louise's child was born dead, and was hastily buried. The details of Rose's death were constantly before Helen, and at times it seemed as if her strength would fail; it seemed impossible that she could nerve herself to the task. But the weeks went by, and it was evident that Louise would live; the recovery was slow, but little by little her strength returned to her. One day Helen paid an early visit to Louise and found her very blue and hysterical. Helen proposed a trip to Europe; not a flying trip, but a visit of, at least, a year, when she could rest at some of those quiet, beautiful spots out of the reach of the usual tourist.

"I shall make Mr. Skidmore go with you," Helen said. Mrs. Skidmore smiled wearily.

"What?"

"Oh, yes."

"He might take me across and fly back again on the next steamer, but you don't think for an instant he'd have time to stay with me?" Helen nodded. "What, a year? I thought you knew better than that, doctor; I assure you it's impossible."

"Very well, I shall do my best. I shall prescribe it as a cure for you. I shall insist; you know I am so very forcible when I insist." Mrs. Skidmore smiled, then she burst into tears, and totally unable to control herself, she sobbed bitterly for some time. Helen prescribed a quieting dose, and returned to her office. As she left the room, she could catch the words, "if you only knew, if you only knew," and Helen in her heart answered, "I know very much more than you dream I know, poor thing."

In her office Helen took up the paper and prepared for a few minutes' rest. Almost the first heading that attracted her attention was.

GREAT DINNER.

The Honorable Harold Skidmore Makes a Powerful
Speech—He Says the Lack of Family life is the
Chief Misery and Degradation of the Poor—Flies
to Philadelphia—Returns to New York by Midnight
Train.

She read on; the speech was extensively quoted:

> The family is the basis of the social structure to-day.…
> The family is an institution, as someone has well said,
> "In whose sacredness we believe society's pillars rest."
> The hopelessness of the present condition of the poor
> lies in the utter absence of family life.… Our problem
> is to build up a pure, a beautiful home life among the
> poor classes, but before we can do that philanthropy
> must step in and supply such influences as are lacking
> at the present moment.
>
> We must never intrude brutally upon the family
> circle of the poor. There is too much of this well-
> meaning but offensive prying into their conditions.
> The man who breaks up the sanctity of home life, who
> destroys the beautiful relation of husband and wife, of
> parents and children, who does anything to weaken
> these blessed ties is sinful, I may say criminal. (Cheers).

More than once during the day was Helen called upon to
discuss the great speech of the night before. On all sides she heard

enthusiastic references. "How true!" "How beautiful!" "How admirably put!"

XVII

When his wife was well enough to take her first drive, Harold called upon Helen. This time he was not kept waiting. He was ushered upstairs into the parlor, which was lit with the soft glow of several shaded lamps. There were cozy easy chairs and small tables filled with odd knick-knacks; one table was entirely for old silver, quite like the collections of a fashionable woman.

Helen entered, dressed in a light, flowing house dress. Harold had not seen her so beautiful for many years; lately he had seen her only in the midst of her professional work—to-night she looked like a queenly woman of the world. Her blond hair was twisted softly, instead of arranged in the smooth straight braids she had accustomed him to lately; her gown had a graceful train, and a profusion of soft yellow lace about her throat softened all the stern lines of her face. In her professional relations she always wore a plain black dress, generally alpaca, short and stiff, and large, wide, flat shoes, while to-night she had on pretty kid slippers, and her foot looked small and well shaped. Dr. Brent was nearly completely lost in the Helen of old. Harold put out his hand impetuously.

"Helen," he said. "I have come to thank you for what you have done for me!" The tears came into her eyes as she grasped his hand. It was years since he had called her anything but doctor. Besides, she had really done so little; what was the saving of his wife's body unless she could save her soul, and she was not sure that she could do that. She was keeping a sharp watch on the movements of Verplanck; she had heard only a day or two ago that he was down South, so she thought there was little to fear from him. Her plan was to send Mrs. Skidmore off to Europe and to try to build up her nervous system by degrees. It would be slow work, but she felt that was the first step and nothing could be done until then. Ultimately she hoped to bring husband and wife together again and to lead her to confess all to him.

They sat there for some time in silence. The thoughts of both reverted to the past. Harold had grown much older; it was evident that great cares sat upon him. The hair about his high white forehead had turned quite gray, the forehead was seamed with many a deep furrow, the mouth had deep lines about it; still the same bright eyes looked at her. How she longed to be able to lay her head upon his shoulder and cry out, "Take me back, take me back." And this man was another's husband, and this other woman had not known how to prize him. "O Harold," she whispered in her heart, "could I have done you a wrong such as this; could I, with all my peculiar views of marriage, could I have so forgotten my wifely duties?"

Something like a groan broke from Helen's lips, and she hastened to break the silence which was growing unbearable. A wild fear possessed her that she would shriek out something that she had no right to say.

"Harold," she said, "you must not thank me; you do not know, indeed, you do not, how much comfort it has been to me that your wife has recovered."

"Helen, I have not only come to thank you, but also to confess my mistake."

"What mistake?" she stammered.

"Yes; I feel truly humble; I, who laughed at your profession, or rather who thought you should leave your work to be done better by men; I, who asked you to give up this work for me; I, who—oh, you know what I mean, Helen—it is hardly necessary for me to speak; it seems almost more than I can bear, when I realize that it is to you I owe the life of my wife. I feel that you did for her what no one else could have done."

"You need not feel humbled for that."

"Yes; I feel humbled to think that I should have dared in my youthful conceit to put myself up against all that your profession must have meant to you. Now, do you understand how I feel? It is a great triumph for you, Helen?" Helen's voice came forth strangely dull and weak.

"No, Harold, it is no triumph for me." She longed to cry out, "Ask me now to give it all up, even now, when you see how much it means; even now, when you know that the world has a claim upon me, ask me now." What she did say was, "I knew some day your better self would understand me and cease to blame me."

"To blame you? You don't know how long ago I ceased to blame you; almost against my will I was forced to acknowledge that you were right, but then I thought myself right too. I looked upon the whole struggle as a miserable problem that never could be solved aright. I do not see that it can. It still seems to me that marriage, as it is on this earth, as it must be, I suppose, cannot mean the union of two such beings as you and I."

"It could, Harold, if you men had faith."

"I see no way out of it, but I have come to acknowledge that it is hard for the woman to sacrifice so much in order to reach her intellectual ideal."

"It is no more necessary for a woman to give it up than a man."

"What?"

"I repeat: there are some things that a man ought to give up just as much as a woman. Only the shoe that pinches has always been supposed to sit on the other foot. You know what Dorothea Brooke says about marriage—'Marriage is a state of higher duties. I never thought of it as mere personal ease.' I am afraid that means that marriage must be a state of higher duties to both man and woman; it is only when both sexes understand the responsibility which rests on each, it is only then that marriage can be truly ideal. Now I am going to give you an evidence of what I mean. Suppose that I absolutely demand that your wife go abroad for at least a year?"

"I should say, by all means, I think it is a good idea."

"Very good. And suppose that I also absolutely demand that your wife goes to Europe accompanied by her husband?"

Harold jumped nearly out of his seat. "Impossible!" he exclaimed.

"That is just what I knew you would say, and yet you will go."

"I cannot. It is impossible; that is too much to ask. I will join her in a few months and remain a month or so with her during the summer."

"No, that is not sufficient; you must accompany her over and remain with her."

"Helen, you are unreasonable. Here's that big railroad case coming off in the courts next month."

"I know it.

"Don't you know I'm pledged to speak at the Republican convention in the spring?"

"Yes, I know it."

"Besides, the President has sent for me; I shall probably be called for, on and off, to Washington during the next six weeks. You know my relations with him are such that I—I—"

"I know it all, but you must go with your wife."

Harold walked about the room impatiently. "Helen, this is pure nonsense; I cannot go, and there's an end to it. I'll engage trained nurses, companions, maids, even a physician. By the way, Helen, why don't you go with her? You could look after her, and she would be very happy with you. By Jove, do you know it would be a capital idea?"

"No trained nurse, companion, or physician is needed. What my patient requires is—a husband." Harold looked at Helen very sharply.

"Why, Helen, what on earth do you mean?"

"I mean that her nerves are completely shattered, that she is utterly broken down, that she ought to have your companionship, your protection, your constant presence. You ought to give up some of these important things that prevent you from being with her." Harold was silent for some time; then he said, with some emotion:

"Perhaps you are right, Helen. I will try to be with her more. Perhaps she has been a little lonely sometimes, poor little woman. I will give up some of my work." Helen's heart gave a great bound. There was a trembling eagerness in her voice as she asked:

"At once? Will you go with her to Europe?"

"Now, Helen, you can't expect a man to reform all at once. My word is given that I will see through some matters personally. When I can get free, I give you my word of honor, the instant I can get free, I shall join my wife in Europe, and will even take a vacation of some months, if necessary. But that will mean that I must wind up some of my affairs. My partners must consent; they must be prepared; then I will go."

"Yes, if not too late," murmured Helen, but she was not heard.

XVIII

There they were, those odious words; there were the lines, black with printers' ink and big, so all the world would be attracted! The words danced before Helen's eyes and her hands trembled so that the paper rattled merrily, but she could just make out the story. There was no mistake; there was no possible chance of mistaken identity; the journalists knew their trade too well, and made sure that everyone would understand the full significance of this latest and spiciest scandal.

ELOPEMENT IN THE FOUR HUNDRED.

Three Hundred and Ninety-eight Shocked and
Horrified—The Wife of the Honorable Harold
Skidmore runs off to Europe with the Heir of the
Verplanck Millions—Rumors that Mr. Skidmore is
Utterly Prostrated—Refuses to be Interviewed.

Mrs. Keith-Brew was ushered into the office. She began at once:

"Why, my dear doctor, you seem quite upset. Yes, I know; isn't it awful! Poor Mr. Skidmore, and yet I don't think anyone else is really surprised." Helen's voice shook.

"Yes, Mrs. Keith-Brew, it is shocking. I am completely overcome. You know Mrs. Skidmore was a patient of mine." The eyes of her visitor twinkled. She knew something now of Helen's story, and she chuckled to herself as she thought that the interest didn't lie on *that* side of the house.

"Well," she answered, demurely, "there's a lot of fuss now, of course, but I suppose there'll be a divorce and then the next thing we hear, Lady Milminme will be entertaining her new sister-in-law at Grey Oaks."

Helen shuddered; she knew how natural that was.

"And I suppose she will be received everywhere," she exclaimed, coldly. Mrs. Keith-Brew laughed disagreeably.

"Well, of course, society can't afford to slight Lady Milminme's sister-in-law. However, we must put on our sternest look until she really is her sister-in-law."

Helen clasped her trembling fingers about her forehead. She leaned back quietly a minute, while her patient eyed her sharply, preparing her account of how Dr. Brent stood the news. Helen's voice was harsh.

"I suppose you and all her dearest friends would cut her now if you met her." Mrs. Keith-Brew looked shocked:

"Why, of course, I hope we have some self-respect left."

"Yesterday you were a good friend of Mrs. Skidmore." Mrs. Keith-Brew smiled.

"Ah, but yesterday was not to-day." She pointed significantly at the paper which lay on the table.

"Ah, yes; I understand; yet you have told me again and again that all the world knew their relations and that people had almost begun to wonder how her husband could be so blind."

"Oh, of course we knew it, but then as long as her husband up-held her and she was received, why I for one wouldn't be the first to push her down. I don't believe in women being too hard upon each other; it's a hard world."

"No, Mrs. Keith-Brew, I don't believe in women being hard upon each other either, but I confess the ways of society have always been darkly mysterious to me; you call it pushing a woman down to show your disapproval before the final crime. Now I have always claimed that the present indifferent attitude of society is the very thing that pushes women down. A woman is indiscreet, she is talked about, and there are shrugs and smiles, but so long as she manages to fool her husband and keep up appearances society refuses to step in. Suddenly she loses her husband's confidence by some flagrantly foolish act, perhaps no worse, but more careless than the others, and the whole world which has been smiling and chattering with her, turns its back and frowns—it knows her no longer."

"But, my dear, you wouldn't have us listen to every bit of idle gossip and be unjust to someone, would you?"

"There is no question of your *listening* to gossip. You not only do that, but you repeat it and enjoy it. It seems to me I would either refuse to listen and believe, or believing—yes, I should dare act up to my belief."

"What, cut a woman for a mere peccadillo, and force her into worse."

"That is the usual society point of view. On the contrary, I claim that if the world would frown on peccadilloes, as you kindly call them, many a vain woman would pause and go no farther. As it is now, society, with its smiles and bows up to the last moment of endurance, only smooths the way down to the lowest pit of shame. A woman like Louise Skidmore—a society queen until to-day—positively goes to her disgrace with the courtesies and applause of society. With all the talk and gossip, the secret sneers that have been going on during the past months, who weren't glad to have

Mrs. Harold Skidmore at their receptions? Oh, it is cruel! Louise Skidmore was weak and foolish, she had few interests to save her, and her husband was unable to shield her as he might have done; yet perhaps if society had dared to say 'This is wrong' when she first began to depend on the society and attention of another than her husband, it might not have been too late. Now, the world may do as it pleases; the mischief is done, done, done."

XIX

It was postmarked Egypt. "I have been ill, [the letter read] very
ill. I think they did not expect me to live one year ago. I was
ordered here for rest and recuperation, 'as if the outside world can
bring back my inward peace of mind,' thought I at first, superbly
indifferent. But day by day, week by week I have grown stronger,
almost against my will. We are animals after all, and we can't resist
physical influences, shrink as we may in the depths of our soul.

"I want to tell you, Helen, I thought I was humbled when
I came to you last to confess, as I thought, poor fool! my mistake.
Humbled! my God! I knew not what the word meant. I was a very
prince of arrogance. If you saw me now, you would not need to ask;
it is written all over my face, on every line of my figure.

"Yes, I understand now. But how was I to know? You tried
to tell me; tried to make me understand. Ah, but the tragedy of
human life is just that each individual being must learn its own
lesson, in its own way, as God sees fit. (A few months ago, Helen,
I could not have used that name.) Was there anything in the lives
of other men about me to make me pause? Nothing; I only did
what hundreds of men were doing, are doing. Why, then, was *I*
singled out for punishment? But this is not the spirit in which I
took up my pen. I have not addressed you to repine, nor to sigh,
nor to curse, but to tell you I see my own life as it was; my own
personality seems to have fallen from me by some mysterious
process, and I can stand aside, almost calmly now, and review the
past.

"How you must smile to see me thus brought so low—but no. I did not mean to write that. You will not smile; you are kind. I remember, last time we met, you said, 'It is no triumph for me, Harold' There was a look in your eyes then, Helen—a look—but I dare not trust to my senses; no, I suppose I am dreaming.

"Why are you so immaculate? Why do I see you before me, armed with righteous indignation? Why does my heart sink so when I try to make believe that there is some flaw, something lacking in your life? Is there room for any regret, for any longing in a life so beautifully full and rich? If I could believe it, and with your last words to me and that look in your eyes, Helen, I might, I might—

"And yet a woman has no right, *no right, I tell you,* to be so faultless, so erect, so self-dependent. It is the province of woman to be humble. You remember *D'Arcy* in the 'Abbesse de Jouarre.'

"Que les anciens maîtres avaient raison de croire que la vertu d'une femme a toujours besoin d'être humiliée; l'humiliation est nécessaire à la femme. La nature l'a voulu.

"This is rank egotism, is it not? But how can I ever hope to explain myself, to portray all that is surging up within me?

"There is a ray of hope that penetrates down to the depths of my heart, a hope that some day I may be able to face the future, to start life over again. It can never be built up again upon the same lines; what I have lived through must prevent that forever.

"So you have not triumphed; life has not poured all its blessings upon you? Bless you for having said that, Helen, bless you! Not now, not now, but some day there will come knocking at your gates a broken Harold, as a suppliant will he come, hat off, eyes lowered, kneeling in the dust."

Appendices

From *Sex in Education*

Or, A Fair Chance for Girls[1]

Edward H. Clarke

"Et l'on nous persuadera difficilement que lorsque
les hommes ont tant de peine à être hommes, les
femmes puissent, tont en restant femmes, devenir
hommes aussi, mettant ainsi la main sur les deux
rôles, exerçant la double mission, résumant le
double caractère de l'humanité! Nous perdrons la
femme, et nous n'aurons pas l'homme. Voila ce qui
nons arrivera. On nous donnera ce quelque chose
de monstreux, cet être répugnant, qui déjà parait à
notre horizon."
—Le Comte A. De Gasparin

"Facts given in evidence are premises from which
a conclusion is to be drawn. The first step in the
exercise of this duty is to acquire a belief of the
truth of the facts."
—Ram, *On Facts*

---

[1] Published by Houghton Mifflin Company—The Riverside Press
(Boston), 1884. [Originally published by James R. Osgood and Company
(Boston), 1873.]

Chiefly Clinical

Clinical observation confirms the teachings of physiology. The sick chamber, not the schoolroom; the physician's private consultation, not the committee's public examination; the hospital, not the college, the workshop, or the parlor,—disclose the sad results which modern social customs, modern education, and modern ways of labor, have entailed on women. Examples of them may be found in every walk of life. On the luxurious couches of Beacon Street; in the palaces of Fifth Avenue; among the classes of our private, common, and normal schools; among the female graduates of our colleges; behind the counters of Washington Street and Broadway; in our factories, workshops, and homes,—may be found numberless pale, weak, neuralgic, dyspeptic, hysterical, menorraghic, dysmenorrhoeic girls and women, that are living illustrations of the truth of this brief monograph. It is not asserted here that improper methods of study, and a disregard of the reproductive apparatus and its functions, during the educational life of girls, are the sole causes of female diseases; neither is it asserted that all the female graduates of our schools and colleges are pathological specimens. But it is asserted that the number of these graduates who have been permanently disabled to a greater or less degree by these causes is so great, as to excite the gravest alarm, and to demand the serious attention of the community. If these causes should continue for the next half-century, and increase in the same ratio as they have for the last fifty years, it requires no prophet to foretell that the wives who are to be mothers in our republic must be drawn from trans-atlantic homes. The sons of the New World will have to react, on a magnificent scale, the old story of unwived Rome and the Sabines.

We have previously seen that the blood is the life, and that the loss of it is the loss of so much life. Deluded by strange theories, and groping in physiological darkness, our fathers' physicians were too often Sangrados. Nourishing food, pure air, and haematized blood were stigmatized as the friends of disease and the enemies of convalescence. Oxygen was shut out from and carbonic acid shut into the passed by. Air and food and blood are recognized as Nature's restoratives. No physician would dare, nowadays, to bleed either man or woman once a month, year in and year out, for a quarter of a century continuously. But girls often have the courage, or the ignorance, to do this to themselves. And the worst of it is, that the organization of our schools and workshops, and the demands of social life and polite society, encourage them in this slow suicide. It has already been stated that the excretory organs, by constantly eliminating from the system its effete and used material, the measure and source of its force, keep the machine in clean, healthy, and working order, and that the reproductive apparatus of woman uses the blood as one of its agents of elimination. Kept within natural limits, this elimination is a source of strength, a perpetual fountain of health, a constant renewal of life. Beyond these limits it is a hemorrhage, that, by draining away the life, becomes a source of weakness and a perpetual fountain of disease.

[...]

This case needs very little comment: its teachings are obvious. Miss D— went to college in good physical condition. During the four years of her college life, her parents and the college faculty required her to get what is popularly called an education. Nature required her, during the same period, to build and put in working-order a large and complicated reproductive mechanism, a matter that is popularly ignored,—shoved out of sight like a disgrace. She naturally obeyed the requirements of the faculty, which she could see, rather than the requirements of the mechanism within her, that she could not see. Subjected to the college regimen, she worked four years in getting a liberal education. Her way of work was sustained and continuous, and out of harmony with the rhythmical periodicity of the female organization. The stream of vital and constructive force evolved within her was turned steadily to the brain, and away from the ovaries and their accessories. The result of this sort of education was, that these last-mentioned organs, deprived of sufficient opportunity and nutriment, first began to perform their functions with pain, a warning of error that was unheeded; then, to cease to grow;[2] next, to set up once a month a grumbling torture that made life miserable; and, lastly, the brain and the whole nervous system, disturbed, in obedience to the law, that, if one member suffers, all the members suffer, became neuralgic and hysterical. And so Miss D— spent the few years next succeeding her graduation in conflict with dysmenorrhoea, headache, neuralgia, and hysteria. Her parents marvelled at her ill-health; and she furnished another text for the often-repeated sermon on the delicacy of American girls.

---

[2] The arrest of development of the uterus, in connection with amenorrhoea, is sometimes very marked. In the New York Medical Journal for June, 1873, three such cases are recorded, that came under the eye of those excellent observers, Dr. E.R. Peaslee and Dr. T.G. Thomas. In one of these cases, the uterine cavity measured one and a half inches; in another, one and seven-eighths inches; and, in a third, one and a quarter inches. Recollecting that the normal measurement is from two and a half to three inches, it appears that the arrest of development in these cases occurred when the uterus was half or less than half grown. Liberal education should avoid such errors.

[...]

The cases which have hitherto been presented illustrate
some of the evils which the reproductive system is apt to receive in
consequence of obvious derangement of its growth and functions.
But it may, and often does, happen that the catamenia are normally
performed, and that the reproductive system is fairly made up
during the educational period. Then force is withdrawn from the
brain and nerves and ganglia. These are dwarfed or checked or
arrested in their development. In the process of waste and repair,
of destructive and constructive metamorphosis, by which brains
as well as bones are built up and consolidated, education often
leaves insufficient margin for growth income derived from air,
food, and sleep, which should largely, may only moderately exceed
expenditure upon study and work, and so leave but little surplus
for growth in any direction; or, what more commonly occurs, the
income which the brain receives is all spent upon study, and little
or none upon its development, while that which the nutritive and
reproductive systems receive is retained by them, and devoted
to their own growth. When the school makes the same steady
demand for force from girls who are approaching puberty, ignoring
Nature's periodical demands, that it does from boys, who are not
called upon for an equal effort, there must be failure somewhere.
Generally either the reproductive system or the nervous system
suffers. We have looked at several instances of the former sort of
failure; let us now examine some of the latter.

From *Sex and Education*

A Reply to Dr. E.H. Clarke's
"Sex in Education"[1]

Julia Ward Howe

When a book challenges public attention to its especial object and intention, we may not inappropriately deal with it before we consider its author. As to the book, then, called "Sex in Education," let us endeavor to make up our minds concerning its character, before we pass on to deal with the topics it suggests.

Is the book, then, a work of science, of literature, or of philosophy, or is it a simple practical treatise on the care of health? We should call it none of these. It has neither the impartiality of science, the form of literature, the breadth of philosophy, nor the friendliness of counsel. It is a work of the polemic type, presenting a persistent and passionate plea against the admission of women to a collegiate education in common with men. The advisableness of such education in common is a question upon which people differ greatly in opinion. So many people of conscience and intelligence hold opposite theories concerning this, that it may be considered as a question fairly open to discussion, and asking to be tested in the light of experience. Dr. Clarke supports his side of the argument by

---

[1] Published by Roberts Brothers (Boston), 1874.

a statement of facts insufficient for his purpose, and by reasonings and inferences irrelevant to the true lesson of these facts. He makes in the first place a strange confusion between things present, past, and future, and in the terror of the identical education to come sees identical education of the sexes in the past and present as the cause of all the ills that female flesh is heir to. He asserts the fact of an ascertained and ever increasing deterioration in the persons of American women from the true womanly standard. He finds them tending ever more and more towards a monstrous type, sterile and sexless; and these facts, which some of us may strongly doubt, he considers accounted for by the corresponding fact that boys and girls receive the same intellectual education. According to him, you cannot feed a woman's brain without starving her body. Brain and body are set in antagonism over against each other, and what is one organ's meat is another's poison. Single women of the intellectual type he characterizes very generally, not only as *agamai*, but as *agenes;* and his portraiture of them is sufficiently revolting. The powerful influence of climate is lightly estimated by him. One hundred years would be insufficient to change the stout, heavily boned English or Irish woman, with her abundant covering of flesh, into the wiry, nervous Yankee woman, characterized by nerve and brain. The cause of all this, of the undeveloped busts, fragile figures, and uncertain health of American women, resides in the fact that with us, as he says, girls and boys receive the same education.

The periodical function peculiar to women is a point upon which Dr. Clarke dwells with persistent iteration. Its neglect he considers the principal source of disease among the women of our land. Its repression or over-production are equally fatal to health; and, in the years which nature consecrates to its establishment, the recurrence of the function should be observed by the avoidance of bodily and mental fatigue. Dr. Clarke's reasoning upon this point affirms that American women neglect care in this direction beyond all other women, and that the school education which our girls receive is the moving cause of this neglect.

We cannot remember a single point in Dr. Clarke's diagnosis of American female hygiene which is not included in the present rapid *résumé*. The Doctor's prognosis is even more dismal and unpromising. Open the doors of your colleges to women, and you will accomplish the ruin of the Commonwealth. Disease—already, according to him, the rule among them—will become without exception. Your girls will lose their physical stature, and your boys their mental stature, since the tasks set for the latter would be limited by the periodical disability of the girls. The result will be a physical and sexual chaos, out of which the Doctor sees no escape save in an act akin to the rape of the Sabines. Tennyson's line suits with his mood:—

"I will take some savage woman, she shall rear my
dusky race."

A number of persons have commented wisely and wittily upon this book and its contents. There is, perhaps, no need of any further detailed criticism of its scope and statement. We have endeavored to give its sense and spirit in little. And we will supplement this synopsis by giving as briefly our own impressions concerning these.

To begin with the observance of the periodical function. This is a good old grandmotherly doctrine, handed down from parent to child through all the ages of humanity. Ignorance of the laws of health would, no doubt, in all ages, induce young persons to disregard the cautions of their elders on this as on other points; and the sharp proverb which tells what young people think of old people, and what the latter know of the former, must often recur to the minds of elderly women preaching care and prudence to daughters and nieces. On the whole, if a pretty wide and long personal experience can go for any thing, I incline to think that the elder generation is much more careful of this point of health than of any other. Many young women who are allowed to eat, dress, live, and behave as they like, are periodically kept from all violent exercise and fatigue, so far as the vigilance of elders can accomplish this. The wilfulness and ingenuity of the young, however, are often more than a match for this vigilance; and a single ride on horseback, a single wetting of the feet, or indulgence in the irresistible German, may entail lifelong misery, which the maternal or friendly guardian has done all in her power to prevent. I myself once knew a German lady who, married and childless for many years, confessed to me that a ball attended in her early youth was the cause of this misfortune.

I have known of repeated instances of incurable disease and even of death arising from rides on horseback taken at the critical period. I have known fatal pulmonary consumption to arise from exposure of the feet in silk stockings, at winter parties. Every matron knows and relates these sad facts to the young girls under her charge. They are sometimes heeded, oftener not. Nothing in our knowledge of youth would lead us to consider them as of rare occurrence. And yet Dr. Clarke attributes most failures of the function and its concomitant, maternity, to the school education received by our girls.

The accusation then of systematic neglect of the periodic function by the educators of youth among us cannot be admitted without more evidence than Dr. Clarke has thus far given us. That women in America particularly neglect their health, that women violate the laws of their constitution as men cannot violate theirs, and that the love of intellectual pursuits causes them to do so, this is the fable out of which Dr. Clarke draws the moral that women must not go to college with men. Fable and moral appear equally unsubstantial. If Dr. Clarke had said that the best men and women of the State, the wisest and noblest, should never allow this subject of education to pass out of their minds or out of their care; if he had said that, after worthily receiving education, the first duty of man and woman is to secure it to the succeeding generation, he would have pointed to the true remedy for all that is amiss on this head. The great increase in the study of physiology among us, and especially among women, must tend, we are sure, to a wiser and better self-culture and care of the young. Education is necessarily "line upon line and precept upon precept." The elder generation can only do its best, and trust to the docility and good faith of the young.

The special character of Dr. Clarke's book provokes the question whether he has not unduly specialized facts which are general, and not limited to any coincidence with that which he especially attacks,—the education of American women, and their physique as affected by it. Is it wholly or principally in America that young women fail of sexual development, have imperfect busts, are afflicted with ill-health and insanity, and in marriage are sterile, or if they have children cannot nurse them?

A well-known sentence of Solomon's shows that even in his time the female form sometimes failed of completeness. Rousseau says of one of the women whom he admired, "*et de la gorge comme de ma main*," with a general slur upon all women so formed.

In Paris has been invented and advertised an artificial bosom warranted to palpitate for a whole evening. It is not likely that this invention has been patented for the exclusive use of American women.

To return to Biblical times, one of the persons healed by our Saviour was a woman suffering from what Dr. Clarke would call *menorrhoea*. It may be as well to remark by the way that during the twelve years of her suffering she had spent all that she had upon physicians, and still was nothing the better, but rather the worse. Sterility was common in the times both of the Old and of the New Testament. It is common to-day among the savages of Africa. It is by no means true that the women who themselves show the greatest physical development are always those whose offspring are the most numerous and healthy. Slender women are often more successful mothers and nurses than the stout sisters whose full outlines attest their own robusticity. Even as to the facts of nursing, women with small breasts often have an abundant supply of milk; while women with fuller outward development often have little or none.

Andrew Combe in his book on Infancy speaks of the great number of infants who in Germany are brought up by hand. He gives most careful rules for rearing infants on artificial food, and does not treat this as at all an uncommon necessity. English women confined in Italy and other foreign countries proverbially lose their milk, and the profession of wet-nurse to an English family has long been one of the most common in Rome and Naples. Many German women in America are obliged to feed their infants wholly or in part, and many American women are good nurses and prolific mothers.

Again we see in Paris papers advertisements of the new remedies, "which the patient herself can apply, and which will

spare her the unpleasant necessity of examinations," &c. Physicians
of large practice and experience are able, in all parts of the world, to
chronicle many cases of uterine disease, of functional derangement,
and of arrested development among women, in which cases no
plea of excessive cerebral action induced by over-study is at all
admissible. But Dr. Clarke sees disease chiefly in American women.
In them reside leucorrhoea, dysmenorrhoea, amenorrhoea, &c. In
them are *ateknia, agalactia, amazia*. And the reason why they have
all these evils is simply this, some of them wish to enter Harvard
College, and some of them have already passed through other
colleges.

Now that the topics of sex and education need careful study
and remodelling of ideas and methods, nobody is less disposed
to deny than the writer of these lines. She is perfectly sure that
the philosophy of sex is thus far little understood in America,
or anywhere else. She has the same impression concerning the
philosophy of education. The physical evils attendant upon the
female constitution are as old as that constitution itself. They
deserve and require the most careful investigation. But the feminine
hygiene will be higher and more complete when it is administered
by women. Personal experience adds an important element even to
the closest and most scientific observation.

Before this pet theory of the incompatibility of health
with intellectual activity, for women only, was discovered, men
of science speculated concerning the deficient busts of American
women. The dry, stimulating climate was supposed, in a great
measure, to account for it. The fact itself reaches back to the
grandmothers of the grandmothers of to-day. It was and is chiefly
observable in the northern and eastern States. As you go south,
you find fuller forms, but not always combined with emptier

heads. The effect of the climate of this portion of the country upon the masculine physique is equally noticeable, and has long been a subject of remark. Men here are for the most part wiry, sinewy, nervous, and brainy. If any of us, carrying out Dr. Clarke's views, prefer to mate with men in whom flesh and muscle counterpoise the tyrannous nerve system, we too must go over the borders, and bring the progenitors of the future race from lands where the east wind blows not. But this reminds us of the well-known overplus of sixty thousand single women in Massachusetts alone. Dr. Clarke arraigns the mothers, actual and possible, for being no better than they are. But what is he going to do about the impossible fathers, in view of the coming generation to which he is so devoted?

If one thing could be more astonishing than another in Dr. Clarke's treatment of his subject, we should give the palm to his consideration of the influence of climate on the human organism. He is unwilling to consider it at all as a factor in the alleged ill-health of American women. According to him one hundred years are not enough to mould the European organism in accordance with the American type. If this is really his opinion, his experience must have differed widely from that of others. I have observed important effects of modification produced by climate, in shorter periods of time than this. Two brothers of one family, resident in Boston, separated at the conclusion of the Revolutionary War. One remained in this city, one migrated to Nova Scotia. Those who at a later day were able to compare the children of these two gentlemen found the Boston family marked with every characteristic of the New England race, thin, nervous, wiry, alert, intense. The Nova Scotian family were stout, full-blooded, and plethoric, altogether of the English colonial type.

English families resident in India soon lose the freshness of their coloring and the fulness of their outline. In fact, the adaptation of one nationality to another is sometimes astonishingly rapid. Mr. Burlingame looked almost like a Chinaman before he died. The writer has seen an American official long resident in Turkey whose physiognomy had become entirely that of his adopted country. The potent American climate works quickly in assimilating the foreign material offered to it. Two generations suffice to efface the salient marks of Celtic, Saxon, French, or Italian descent. The Negro alone is able to offer a respectable resistance.

It may occur to some that the assumed identity of the intellectual education given to girls and boys in America may have less to do with the ill-health of the former than the dissimilarity of their physical training. Boys are much in the open air. Girls are much in the house. Boys wear a dress which follows and allows their natural movements. Girls wear clothes which impede and almost paralyze their limbs. Boys have, moreover, the healthful hope held out to them of being able to pursue their own objects, and to choose and follow the business or profession of their choice. Girls have the dispiriting prospect of a secondary and derivative existence, with only so much room allowed them as may not cramp the full sweep of the other sex. The circumstances first named directly affect health, the last exerts a strong reflex action upon it. "We are only women, and it does not matter," passes from mother to daughter. A very estimable young lady said to me the other day, in answer to a plea for dress-reform, "It is better to look handsome, even if it does shorten life a little." Her care of herself probably does not go beyond that indicated by this saying. Dr. Clarke cites a few instances of functional derangement. But by far the most frequent difficulty with our women arises from uterine displacement, and this in turn comes partly from the utter disuse of the muscles which should keep the uterus in place, but which are kept inactive by the corset, weighed upon by the heavy skirt, and drawn upon by the violent and unnatural motion of the dancing at present in vogue. Is it any wonder that these ill-educated, over-burthened muscles give way, like other ill-trained, over-powered things? Some instances of remarkable robustness in women have been the result of a physical education identical with that usually given to boys. In these cases, the parents, after repeated losses of children through much cherishing, have at last determined to give the girls a chance through athletic sports and unrestricted exercise in the open air. And this has again and again proved successful.

Much in Dr. Clarke's treatment of his subject is objectionable. We are left in doubt whether his book was written for men or for women, and we conclude that his method of statement is not good for either. Much of his remarking upon sex is justly offensive, and his statements concerning those single women of culture whom he terms *agenes* would scarcely be endured in any household in which these single saints bear the burthens of all the others, and lead lives divinely wedded to duty. The odious expression which completes his picture of "the girls tied to their dictionaries," &c., would exclude the book, and the writer too, from some pure and polite circles. And we must say to him, with all due regard for the good intentions with which we desire to credit him,—

"These things must not be thought of on this wise."

I have thus attempted a brief addition to the comments of women upon Dr. Clarke's work, telling pretty plainly what I think of it, and why. But a full discussion of these great themes of Sex and Education can hardly be had in answer to a summons so sharp and so partial as his own. Not to dogmatize and counter-dogmatize upon these points will make either men or women wiser. Not for those who think they know every thing about the matter to discourse to those whom they judge as knowing nothing about it. These processes will always retard instead of advancing the discovery of truth. But when men and women may meet together for fair and equal interchange of thought, the men not wanting in modesty, nor the women in courage, then we shall be glad to listen, if we do not speak. And if we do speak, we shall say, "Father, thou hast made all things well, and without thy wisdom was not any thing made that was made."

Hygiene and Morality

A Manual for Nurses and Others, Giving an Outline of the Medical, Social, and Legal Aspects of Venereal Disease[1]

Lavinia Dock

Siphilis

The venereal diseases are, in the commonly accepted order of their gravity: Syphilis; Gonorrhoea; Chancroid. The first mentioned is, by many modern medical writers, classed by itself, as will be explained later. For a long period in medical history, these three were all believed to be manifestations of one and the same disease. This confusion of ideas continued until the identification of the specific causative germs brought definite understanding and gave a sound basis to theory.

Historical Outline. Venereal diseases are of great, probably of unknown antiquity. Some writers say that gonorrhoea has always existed. Syphilis appears to accompany certain stages of civilisation, as at least some barbarous tribes are and have been free from it. It is known that it has been introduced into certain ones of such tribes

---

[1] Published by G.P. Putnam & Sons—The Knickerbocker Press (New York and London), 1910.

by white men. This has recently occurred with decimating results in the case of the tribe of Baganzas in Central Africa.

Some medical historians affirm that syphilis was unknown in Europe before the discovery of America and that it was carried thence into Europe, having presumably had its source in the ancient civilisations of Central America. Prominent authorities hold this view, while others, also prominent, maintain that it has existed for many more centuries in Europe but has been confused with leprosy. The controversy is one of no more than academic interest. What is historically certain is, that an epidemic of syphilis of frightful virulence raged in Europe at the end of the fifteenth century, constituting a veritable plague, and that it spread to all the countries and corners of the continent. Since then, it has been ever present in a less spectacular, sub-acute form as an endemic disease. Though now less noticeable, it is no less pestilential; perhaps indeed it is even more dangerous by reason of its concealment, as it is thus able to promote undiscovered that racial degeneration which has been pointed out as one of its chief activities.

Cause of Syphilis. Syphilis is caused by a micro-organism called the *Spirochoete pallida* of Schaudinn. This micro-organism, the specific and invariable cause of syphilis, has not long been known with certainty, though long before its actual demonstration medical specialists had suspected its existence. Metchnikoff records the work of Donnè, a French microscopist, who, in 1837, tried to learn from his microscope the exact nature of the genito-urinary discharge in both men and women. But his efforts resulted in nothing definite. In his day the germ theory was nonexistent. After the work of Pasteur had given a new direction to medical and surgical study and had caused the doctrine of the action of

micro-organisms as the cause of infectious disease to be accepted,
active search and research went on in laboratories all over the
world, to discover the germs of this as well as of other diseases. But
for twenty years or more the definite attempts made by Weigart,
Lustgarten, Metchnikoff, and many others to find the cause of
syphilis ended in failure. Finally a commission of experts was
formed under the lead of Schulze, Professor of Zoölogy in the
University of Berlin, and the investigation directed toward the
discovery of the syphilitic virus was by him entrusted to Schaudinn
and Hoffman, who, finally, were successful in their search, and
in 1905 were able to demonstrate the micro-organism which is
now generally accepted by the medical profession as the cause of
syphilis.

Underlying Principles of Prevention

Prostitution To Be Prevented. The genuine prevention of venereal
disease is only made possible by the prevention of prostitution.
Prostitution cannot be retained and the diseases fostered in it
be eliminated. Prostitution must be rooted out, unless modern
civilised states are content to look forward to the same fate which
befell ancient Rome.

The English women, as they worked on through their
crusade, came to see what at first they had not realised, that what
they were making war upon was actually the social institution
of prostitution itself. Thirty-five years ago Mrs. Butler said, in a
public address: "That we are, and have been all along, contending
for more than the mere repeal of these unjust and unholy Acts of
Parliament, is proved by certain signs which are becoming more
and more clear and frequent."

Knowledge Is Essential. The first essential in a campaign of
prevention is full, open, and serious instruction for all classes of
society upon the situation as it exists to-day; instruction without
exaggeration, but also without concealment, of the present extent
of disease of venereal origin, and with the most emphatic and
positive information upon the real source of danger in prostitution.
It will be found that not only is the extent to which venereal
diseases have been allowed to prey upon the national stock utterly
undreamed of by great numbers of highly intelligent persons, but
that their very existence is, to thousands of others, only the vaguest
hearsay, while to thousands more absolutely unknown. Now, as in
combating typhoid fever and the plague the first thing needful is
that all shall know that there are such diseases, whence their origin,
and how they may be cut off at their source, so it is essential that
every citizen shall know that there are venereal diseases, where they
arise, and how they may be exterminated.

Therefore, a wide-spread campaign of popular education
must be the first movement made. This has already been begun by
the national societies founded for the purpose, and, as their task is
a most difficult one, they should have the active support of every
right thinking man and woman. Extreme difficulties meet this
movement at the outset, arising from the peculiarly personal origin
of these diseases, the prevailing false modesty as to the reproductive
functions, and the generally dense ignorance of the physiology
and hygiene of the generative organs. The vulgar prudery and
hypocrisy of a past age compelled all such subjects to be tabooed,
as being indelicate or improper. Perhaps this point of view has been
encouraged by those whose interests were selfish or evil; certainly
nothing could better serve such interests than the veil of silence and
the cloak of embarrassment drawn over subjects so vital, pertaining

to functions by nature so sacred, but by man so horribly debased. The function of reproduction, for which the organs of generation have been evolved, though it has been dragged through the mire of vulgar thoughts and cruel abuse, is yet the noblest, as it should be the most held in reverence of all human powers. Reproduction is natural, and should no more be regarded vulgarly than are the changes of the seasons. It is a type and symbol of immortality. It is indeed a present and visible immortality, and its humble physical phenomena should never obscure its exalted significance. The generative act should only be performed in the sincerity of aspiration to bring a new being into the world. Such being the truth, the depravity of exercising so miraculous a power for the sole desire of a passing pleasure of sensation, often combining with it drunkenness, and orgies in which all human dignity and decency are cast away, is so complete that the decay and fall of nations would seem to need no further explanation.

The generative organs do not suffer by non-use. This statement is now being emphasised with great earnestness by our foremost medical teachers. Nor does the general health suffer by their non-use. This is also emphasised, and is the basis of the modern scientific teaching upon sex hygiene that is now being given to young men in the universities of many countries.

It must be seen to that no children are allowed to grow up in the future in ignorance or with secret vulgarised notions of sex physiology. The simple truth, told them little by little from the earliest age at which they begin to ask questions and in a way which will appeal to their idealism; then later teaching in the schools in biology, physiology, and nature study, will go far toward prevention, by introducing a new ideal. The teaching of older boys and girls should point to their responsibilities to future generations.

As a woman physician has well said, young men who might be deaf to the appeal of an individualistic morality may be moved to response by the presentation of their debt to race and country.

The education of fathers and mothers must, in the future, include the principles of heredity, the toxic effect of unholy passions upon temperament and character, and the study of eugenics, the new science for the improvement of the race of man.

First and last, women need to be encouraged to revolt against a status of political and legal inferiority which is the direct cause of their economic and social degradation.

The Hypocrisy of Puritanism [1]

Emma Goldman

Speaking of Puritanism in relation to American art, Mr. Gutzen Burglum said: "Puritanism has made us self-centered and hypocritical for so long, that sincerity and reverence for what is natural in our impulses have been fairly bred out of us, with the result that there can be neither truth nor individuality in our art."

Mr. Burglum might have added that Puritanism has made life itself impossible. More than art, more than estheticism, life represents beauty in a thousand variations; it is, indeed, a gigantic panorama of eternal change. Puritanism, on the other hand, rests on a fixed and immovable conception of life; it is based on the Calvinistic idea that life is a curse, imposed upon man by the wrath of God. In order to redeem himself man must do constant penance, must repudiate every natural and healthy impulse, and turn his back on joy and beauty.

Puritanism celebrated its reign of terror in England during the sixteenth and seventeenth centuries, destroying and crushing every manifestation of art and culture. It was the spirit of Puritanism which robbed Shelley of his children, because he would not bow to the dicta of religion. It was the same narrow spirit

---

[1] Published in Emma Goldman, *Anarchism and Other Essays* (New York: Mother Earth Publishing Association), 1910.

141

which alienated Byron from his native land, because that great
genius rebelled against the monotony, dullness, and pettiness of his
country. It was Puritanism, too, that forced some of England's freest
women into the conventional lie of marriage: Mary Wollstonecraft
and, later, George Eliot. And recently Puritanism has demanded
another toll—the life of Oscar Wilde. In fact, Puritanism has
never ceased to be the most pernicious factor in the domain of
John Bull, acting as censor of the artistic expression of his people,
and stamping its approval only on the dullness of middle-class
respectability.

It is therefore sheer British jingoism which points to America
as the country of Puritanic provincialism. It is quite true that
our life is stunted by Puritanism, and that the latter is killing
what is natural and healthy in our impulses. But it is equally true
that it is to England that we are indebted for transplanting this
spirit on American soil. It was bequeathed to us by the Pilgrim
fathers. Fleeing from persecution and oppression, the Pilgrims of
Mayflower fame established in the New World a reign of Puritanic
tyranny and crime. The history of New England, and especially
of Massachusetts, is full of the horrors that have turned life into
gloom, joy into despair, naturalness into disease, honesty and truth
into hideous lies and hypocrisies. The ducking-stool and whipping
post, as well as numerous other devices of torture, were the favorite
English methods for American purification.

Boston, the city of culture, has gone down in the annals of
Puritanism as the "Bloody Town." It rivaled Salem, even, in her
cruel persecution of unauthorized religious opinions. On the now
famous Common a half-naked woman, with a baby in her arms,
was publicly whipped for the crime of free speech; and on the same
spot Mary Dyer, another Quaker woman, was hanged in 1659. In

fact, Boston has been the scene of more than one wanton crime committed by Puritanism. Salem, in the summer of 1692, killed eighteen people for witchcraft. Nor was Massachusetts alone in driving out the devil by fire and brimstone. As Canning justly said: "The Pilgrim fathers infested the New World to redress the balance of the Old." The horrors of that period have found their most supreme expression in the American classic, *The Scarlet Letter*.

Puritanism no longer employs the thumbscrew and lash; but it still has a most pernicious hold on the minds and feelings of the American people. Naught else can explain the power of a Comstock. Like the Torquemadas of ante-bellum days, Anthony Comstock is the autocrat of American morals; he dictates the standards of good and evil, of purity and vice. Like a thief in the night he sneaks into the private lives of the people, into their most intimate relations. The system of espionage established by this man Comstock puts to shame the infamous Third Division of the Russian secret police. Why does the public tolerate such an outrage on its liberties? Simply because Comstock is but the loud expression of the Puritanism bred in the Anglo-Saxon blood, and from whose thraldom even liberals have not succeeded in fully emancipating themselves. The visionless and leaden elements of the old Young Men's and Women's Christian Temperance Unions, Purity Leagues, American Sabbath Unions, and the Prohibition Party, with Anthony Comstock as their patron saint, are the grave diggers of American art and culture.

Europe can at least boast of a bold art and literature which delve deeply into the social and sexual problems of our time, exercising a severe critique of all our shams. As with a surgeon's knife every Puritanic carcass is dissected, and the way thus cleared for man's liberation from the dead weights of the past. But with

Puritanism as the constant check upon American life, neither truth nor sincerity is possible. Nothing but gloom and mediocrity to dictate human conduct, curtail natural expression, and stifle our best impulses. Puritanism in this the twentieth century is as much the enemy of freedom and beauty as it was when it landed on Plymouth Rock. It repudiates, as something vile and sinful, our deepest feelings; but being absolutely ignorant as to the real functions of human emotions, Puritanism is itself the creator of the most unspeakable vices.

The entire history of asceticism proves this to be only too true. The Church, as well as Puritanism, has fought the flesh as something evil; it had to be subdued and hidden at all cost. The result of this vicious attitude is only now beginning to be recognized by modern thinkers and educators. They realize that "nakedness has a hygienic value as well as a spiritual significance, far beyond its influences in allaying the natural inquisitiveness of the young or acting as a preventative of morbid emotion. It is an inspiration to adults who have long outgrown any youthful curiosities. The vision of the essential and eternal human form, the nearest thing to us in all the world, with its vigor and its beauty and its grace, is one of the prime tonics of life."[2] But the spirit of purism has so perverted the human mind that it has lost the power to appreciate the beauty of nudity, forcing us to hide the natural form under the plea of chastity. Yet chastity itself is but an artificial imposition upon nature, expressive of a false shame of the human form. The modern idea of chastity, especially in reference to woman, its greatest victim, is but the sensuous exaggeration

---

[2] *The Psychology of Sex*. Havelock Ellis.

of our natural impulses. "Chastity varies with the amount of clothing," and hence Christians and purists forever hasten to cover the "heathen" with tatters, and thus convert him to goodness and chastity.

Puritanism, with its perversion of the significance and functions of the human body, especially in regard to woman, has condemned her to celibacy, or to the indiscriminate breeding of a diseased race, or to prostitution. The enormity of this crime against humanity is apparent when we consider the results. Absolute sexual continence is imposed upon the unmarried woman, under pain of being considered immoral or fallen, with the result of producing neurasthenia, impotence, depression, and a great variety of nervous complaints involving diminished power of work, limited enjoyment of life, sleeplessness, and preoccupation with sexual desires and imaginings. The arbitrary and pernicious dictum of total continence probably also explains the mental inequality of the sexes. Thus Freud believes that the intellectual inferiority of so many women is due to the inhibition of thought imposed upon them for the purpose of sexual repression. Having thus suppressed the natural sex desires of the unmarried woman, Puritanism, on the other hand, blesses her married sister for incontinent fruitfulness in wedlock. Indeed, not merely blesses her, but forces the woman, oversexed by previous repression, to bear children, irrespective of weakened physical condition or economic inability to rear a large family. Prevention, even by scientifically determined safe methods, is absolutely prohibited; nay, the very mention of the subject is considered criminal.

Thanks to this Puritanic tyranny, the majority of women soon find themselves at the ebb of their physical resources. Ill and worn, they are utterly unable to give their children even elementary care. That, added to economic pressure, forces many women to risk utmost danger rather than continue to bring forth life. The custom of procuring abortions has reached such vast proportions in America as to be almost beyond belief. According to recent investigations along this line, seventeen abortions are committed in every hundred pregnancies. This fearful percentage represents only cases which come to the knowledge of physicians. Considering the secrecy in which this practice is necessarily shrouded, and the consequent professional inefficiency and neglect, Puritanism continuously exacts thousands of victims to its own stupidity and hypocrisy.

Prostitution, although hounded, imprisoned, and chained, is nevertheless the greatest triumph of Puritanism. It is its most cherished child, all hypocritical sanctimoniousness notwithstanding. The prostitute is the fury of our century, sweeping across the "civilized" countries like a hurricane, and leaving a trail of disease and disaster. The only remedy Puritanism offers for this ill-begotten child is greater repression and more merciless persecution. The latest outrage is represented by the Page Law, which imposes upon New York the terrible failure and crime of Europe; namely, registration and segregation of the unfortunate victims of Puritanism. In equally stupid manner purism seeks to check the terrible scourge of its own creation— venereal diseases. Most disheartening it is that this spirit of obtuse narrow-mindedness has poisoned even our so-called liberals, and has blinded them into joining the crusade against the very things born of the hypocrisy of Puritanism—prostitution and its results. In wilful blindness Puritanism refuses to see that the true method of prevention is the one which makes it clear to all that "venereal diseases are not a mysterious or terrible thing, the penalty of the sin of the flesh, a sort of shameful evil branded by purist malediction, but an ordinary disease which may be treated and cured." By its methods of obscurity, disguise, and concealment, Puritanism has furnished favorable conditions for the growth and spread of these diseases. Its bigotry is again most strikingly demonstrated by the senseless attitude in regard to the great discovery of Prof. Ehrlich, hypocrisy veiling the important cure for syphilis with vague allusions to a remedy for "a certain poison."

The almost limitless capacity of Puritanism for evil is due to its intrenchment behind the State and the law. Pretending to safeguard the people against "immorality," it has impregnated the machinery of government and added to its usurpation of moral guardianship the legal censorship of our views, feelings, and even of our conduct.

Art, literature, the drama, the privacy of the mails, in fact, our most intimate tastes, are at the mercy of this inexorable tyrant. Anthony Comstock, or some other equally ignorant policeman, has been given power to desecrate genius, to soil and mutilate the sublimest creation of nature—the human form. Books dealing with the most vital issues of our lives, and seeking to shed light upon dangerously obscured problems, are legally treated as criminal offenses, and their helpless authors thrown into prison or driven to destruction and death.

Not even in the domain of the Tsar is personal liberty daily outraged to the extent it is in America, the stronghold of the Puritanic eunuchs. Here the only day of recreation left to the masses, Sunday, has been made hideous and utterly impossible. All writers on primitive customs and ancient civilization agree that the Sabbath was a day of festivities, free from care and duties, a day of general rejoicing and merry-making. In every European country this tradition continues to bring some relief from the humdrum and stupidity of our Christian era. Everywhere concert halls, theaters, museums, and gardens are filled with men, women, and children, particularly workers with their families, full of life and joy, forgetful of the ordinary rules and conventions of their every-day existence. It is on that day that the masses demonstrate what life might really mean in a sane society, with work stripped of its profit-making, soul-destroying purpose.

Puritanism has robbed the people even of that one day. Naturally, only the workers are affected: our millionaires have their luxurious homes and elaborate clubs. The poor, however, are condemned to the monotony and dullness of the American Sunday. The sociability and fun of European outdoor life is here exchanged for the gloom of the church, the stuffy, germ-saturated country parlor, or the brutalizing atmosphere of the back-room saloon. In Prohibition States the people lack even the latter, unless they can invest their meager earnings in quantities of adulterated liquor. As to Prohibition, every one knows what a farce it really is. Like all other achievements of Puritanism it, too, has but driven the "devil" deeper into the human system. Nowhere else does one meet so many drunkards as in our Prohibition towns. But so long as one can use scented candy to abate the foul breath of hypocrisy, Puritanism is triumphant. Ostensibly Prohibition is opposed to liquor for reasons of health and economy, but the very spirit of Prohibition being itself abnormal, it succeeds but in creating an abnormal life.

Every stimulus which quickens the imagination and raises the spirits, is as necessary to our life as air. It invigorates the body, and deepens our vision of human fellowship. Without stimuli, in one form or another, creative work is impossible, nor indeed the spirit of kindliness and generosity. The fact that some great geniuses have seen their reflection in the goblet too frequently, does not justify Puritanism in attempting to fetter the whole gamut of human emotions. A Byron and a Poe have stirred humanity deeper than all the Puritans can ever hope to do. The former have given to life meaning and color; the latter are turning red blood into water, beauty into ugliness, variety into uniformity and decay. Puritanism, in whatever expression, is a poisonous germ. On the surface everything may look strong and vigorous; yet the poison works its way persistently, until the entire fabric is doomed. With Hippolyte Taine, every truly free spirit has come to realize that "Puritanism is the death of culture, philosophy, humor, and good fellowship; its characteristics are dullness, monotony, and gloom."

From *The Crux*

A Novel[1]

Charlotte Perkins Gilman

Consequences

You may have a fondness for grapes that are green,
And the sourness that greenness beneath;
You may have a right
To a colic at night—
But consider your children's teeth!

Dr. Hale retired from his gaily illuminated grounds in too much
displeasure to consider the question of dignity. One suddenly
acting cause was the news given him by Vivian. The other was
the sight of Morton Elder's face as he struck a match to light his
cigarette.

Thus moved, and having entered and left his own grounds
like a thief in the night, he proceeded to tramp in the high-lying
outskirts of the town until every light in his house had gone out.
Then he returned, let himself into his office, and lay there on a
lounge until morning.

---

[1] Published by Charlton Company (New York), 1910.

Vivian had come out so quickly to greet the doctor from obscure motives. She felt a sudden deep objection to being found there with Morton, a wish to appear as one walking about unconcernedly, and when that match glow made Morton's face shine out prominently in the dark shelter, she, too, felt a sudden displeasure.

Without a word she went swiftly to the house, excused herself to her Grandmother, who nodded understandingly, and returned to The Cottonwoods, to her room. She felt that she must be alone and think; think of that irrevocable word she had uttered, and its consequences.

She sat at her window, rather breathless, watching the rows of pink lanterns swaying softly on the other side of the street; hearing the lively music, seeing young couples leave the gate and stroll off homeward.

Susie's happiness came more vividly to mind than her own. It was so freshly joyous, so pure, so perfectly at rest. She could not feel that way, could not tell with decision exactly how she did feel. But if this was happiness, it was not as she had imagined it. She thought of that moonlit summer night so long ago, and the memory of its warm wonder seemed sweeter than the hasty tumult and compulsion of to-night.

She was stirred through and through by Morton's intense emotion, but with a sort of reaction, a wish to escape. He had been so madly anxious, he had held her so close; there seemed no other way but to yield to him—in order to get away.

And then Dr. Hale had jarred the whole situation. She had to be polite to him, in his own grounds. If only Morton had kept still—that grating match—his face, bent and puffing, Dr. Hale must have seen him. And again she thought of little Susie with

almost envy. Even after that young lady had come in, bubbled over
with confidences and raptures, and finally dropped to sleep without
Vivian's having been able to bring herself to return the confidences,
she stole back to her window again to breathe.

Why had Dr. Hale started so at the name of Mrs. St. Cloud?
That was puzzling her more than she cared to admit. By and by she
saw his well-known figure, tall and erect, march by on the other
side and go into the office.

"O, well," she sighed at last, "I'm not young, like Susie.
Perhaps it *is* like this—"

Now Morton had been in no special need of that cigarette
at that special moment, but he did not wish to seem to hide in the
dusky arbor, nor to emerge lamely as if he had hidden. So he lit the
match, more from habit than anything else. When it was out, and
the cigarette well lighted, he heard the doctor's sudden thump on
the other side of the fence and came out to rejoin Vivian. She was
not there.

He did not see her again that night, and his meditations
were such that next day found him, as a lover, far more agreeable
to Vivian than the night before. He showed real understanding, no
triumph, no airs of possession; took no liberties, only said: "When
I am good enough I shall claim you—my darling!" and looked at
her with such restrained longing that she quite warmed to him
again.

He held to this attitude, devoted, quietly affectionate; till
her sense of rebellion passed away and her real pleasure in his
improvement reasserted itself. As they read together, if now and
then his arm stole around her waist, he always withdrew it when
so commanded. Still, one cannot put the same severity into a
prohibition too often repeated. The constant, thoughtful attention

of a man experienced in the art of pleasing women, the new and frankly inexperienced efforts he made to meet her highest thoughts, to learn and share her preferences, both pleased her.

He was certainly good looking, certainly amusing, certainly had become a better man from her companionship. She grew to feel a sort of ownership in this newly arisen character; a sort of pride in it. Then, she had always been fond of Morton, since the time when he was only "Susie's big brother." That counted.

Another thing counted, too, counted heavily, though Vivian never dreamed of it and would have hotly repudiated the charge. She was a woman of full marriageable age, with all the unused powers of her woman's nature calling for expression, quite unrecognized.

He was a man who loved her, loved her more deeply than he had ever loved before, than he had even known he could love; who quite recognized what called within him and meant to meet the call. And he was near her every day.

After that one fierce outbreak he held himself well in check. He knew he had startled her then, almost lost her. And with every hour of their companionship he felt more and more how much she was to him. Other women he had pursued, overtaken, left behind. He felt that there was something in Vivian which was beyond him, giving a stir and lift of aspiration which he genuinely enjoyed.

Day by day he strove to win her full approval, and day by day he did not neglect the tiny, slow-lapping waves of little tendernesses, small affectionate liberties at well-chosen moments, always promptly withdrawing when forbidden, but always beginning again a little further on.

Dr. Bellair went to Dr. Hale's office and sat herself down solidly in the patient's chair.

"Dick," she said, "are you going to stand for this?"

"Stand for what, my esteemed but cryptic fellow-practitioner?"

She eyed his calm, reserved countenance with friendly admiration. "You are an awfully good fellow, Dick, but dull. At the same time dull and transparent. Are you going to sit still and let that dangerous patient of yours marry the finest girl in town?"

"Your admiration for girls is always stronger than mine, Jane; and I have, if you will pardon the boast, more than one patient."

"All right, Dick—if you want it made perfectly clear to your understanding. Do you mean to let Morton Elder marry Vivian Lane?"

"What business is it of mine?" he demanded, more than brusquely—savagely.

"You know what he's got."

"I am a physician, not a detective. And I am not Miss Lane's father, brother, uncle or guardian."

"Or lover," added Dr. Bellair, eyeing him quietly. She thought she saw a second's flicker of light in the deep gray eyes, a possible tightening of set lips. "Suppose you are not," she said; "nor even a humanitarian. You *are* a member of society. Do you mean to let a man whom you know has no right to marry, poison the life of that splendid girl?"

He was quite silent for a moment, but she could see the hand on the farther arm of his chair grip it till the nails were white.

"How do you know he wishes to marry her?"

"If you were about like other people, you old hermit, you'd know it as well as anybody. I think they are on the verge of an engagement, if they aren't over it already. Once more, Dick, shall you do anything?"

"No," said he. Then, as she did not add a word, he rose and walked up and down the office in big strides, turning upon her at last.

"You know how I feel about this. It is a matter of honor—professional honor. You women don't seem to know what the word means. I've told that good-for-nothing young wreck that he has no right to marry for years yet, if ever. That is all I can do. I will not betray the confidence of a patient."

"Not if he had smallpox, or scarlet fever, or the bubonic plague? Suppose a patient of yours had the leprosy, and wanted to marry your sister, would you betray his confidence?"

"I might kill my sister," he said, glaring at her. "I refuse to argue with you."

"Yes, I think you'd better refuse," she said, rising. "And you don't have to kill Vivian Lane, either. A man's honor always seems to want to kill a woman to satisfy it. I'm glad I haven't got the feeling. Well, Dick, I thought I'd give you a chance to come to your senses, a real good chance. But I won't leave you to the pangs of unavailing remorse, you poor old goose. That young syphilitic is no patient of mine." And she marched off to perform a difficult duty.

She was very fond of Vivian. The girl's unselfish sweetness of character and the depth of courage and power she perceived behind the sensitive, almost timid exterior, appealed to her. If she had had a daughter, perhaps she would have been like that. If she had had a daughter would she not have thanked anyone who would try to save her from such a danger? From that worse than deadly peril, because of which she had no daughter.

Dr. Bellair was not the only one who watched Morton's growing devotion with keen interest. To his aunt it was a constant joy. From the time her boisterous little nephew had come to rejoice her heart and upset her immaculate household arrangements, and had played, pleasantly though tyrannically, with the little girl next door, Miss Orella had dreamed this romance for him. To have it fail was part of her grief when he left her, to have it now so visibly coming to completion was a deep delight.

If she had been blind to his faults, she was at least vividly conscious of the present sudden growth of virtues. She beamed at him with affectionate pride, and her manner to Mrs. Pettigrew was one of barely subdued "I told you so." Indeed, she could not restrain herself altogether, but spoke to that lady with tender triumph of how lovely it was to have Morton so gentle and nice.

"You never did like the boy, I know, but you must admit that he is behaving beautifully now."

"I will," said the old lady; "I'll admit it without reservation. He's behaving beautifully—now. But I'm not going to talk about him—to you, Orella." So she rolled up her knitting work and marched off.

"Too bad she's so prejudiced and opinionated," said Miss Elder to Susie, rather warmly. "I'm real fond of Mrs. Pettigrew, but when she takes a dislike——"

Susie was so happy herself that she seemed to walk in an aura of rosy light. Her Jimmie was so evidently the incarnation of every masculine virtue and charm that he lent a reflected lustre to other men, even to her brother. Because of her love for Jimmie, she loved Morton better—loved everybody better. To have her only brother marry her dearest friend was wholly pleasant to Susie.

It was not difficult to wring from Vivian a fair knowledge of how things stood, for, though reserved by nature, she was utterly unused to concealing anything, and could not tell an efficient lie if she wanted to.

"Are you engaged or are you not, you dear old thing?" demanded Susie.

And Vivian admitted that there was "an understanding." But Susie absolutely must not speak of it.

For a wonder she did not, except to Jimmie. But people seemed to make up their minds on the subject with miraculous agreement. The general interest in the manifold successes of Mrs. St. Cloud gave way to this vivid personal interest, and it was discussed from two sides among their whole circle of acquaintance.

One side thought that a splendid girl was being wasted, sacrificed, thrown away, on a disagreeable, good-for-nothing fellow. The other side thought the "interesting" Mr. Elder might have done better; they did not know what he could see in her.

They, that vaguely important They, before whom we so deeply bow, were also much occupied in their mind by speculations concerning Mr. Dykeman and two Possibilities. One quite patently possible, even probable, giving rise to the complacent "Why, anybody could see that!" and the other a fascinatingly impossible Possibility of a sort which allows the even more complacent "Didn't you? Why, I could see it from the first."

Mr. Dykeman had been a leading citizen in that new-built town for some ten years, which constituted him almost the Oldest Inhabitant. He was reputed to be extremely wealthy, though he never said anything about it, and neither his clothing nor his cigars reeked of affluence. Perhaps nomadic chambermaids had spread knowledge of those silver-backed appurtenances, and the long mirror. Or perhaps it was not woman's gossip at all, but men's gossip, which has wider base, and wider circulation, too.

Mr. Dykeman had certainly "paid attentions" to Miss Elder. Miss Elder had undeniably brightened and blossomed most becomingly under these attentions. He had danced with her, he had driven with her, he had played piquet with her when he might have played whist. To be sure, he did these things with other ladies, and had done them for years past, but this really looked as if there might be something in it.

Mr. Skee, as Mr. Dykeman's oldest friend, was even questioned a little; but it was not very much use to question Mr. Skee. His manner was not repellant, and not in the least reserved. He poured forth floods of information so voluminous and so varied that the recipient was rather drowned than fed. So opinions wavered as to Mr. Dykeman's intentions.

Then came this lady of irresistible charm, and the unmarried citizens of the place fell at her feet as one man. Even the married ones slanted over a little.

Mr. Dykeman danced with her, more than he had with Miss Elder. Mr. Dykeman drove with her, more than he had with Miss Elder. Mr. Dykeman played piquet with her, and chess, which Miss Elder could not play. And Miss Elder's little opening petals of ribbon and lace curled up and withered away; while Mrs. St. Cloud's silken efflorescence, softly waving and jewel-starred, flourished apace.

Dr. Bellair had asked Vivian to take a walk with her; and they sat together, resting, on a high lonely hill, a few miles out of town.

"It's a great pleasure to see this much of you, Dr. Bellair," said the girl, feeling really complimented.

"I'm afraid you won't think so, my dear, when you hear what I have to say: what I *have* to say."

The girl flushed a little. "Are you going to scold me about something? Have I done anything wrong?" Her eyes smiled bravely. "Go on, Doctor. I know it will be for my best good."

"It will indeed, dear child," said the doctor, so earnestly that Vivian felt a chill of apprehension.

"I am going to talk to you 'as man to man' as the story books say; as woman to woman. When I was your age I had been married three years."

Vivian was silent, but stole out a soft sympathetic hand and slipped it into the older woman's. She had heard of this early-made marriage, also early broken; with various dark comments to which she had paid no attention.

Dr. Bellair was Dr. Bellair, and she had a reverential affection for her.

There was a little silence. The Doctor evidently found it hard to begin. "You love children, don't you, Vivian?"

The girl's eyes kindled, and a heavenly smile broke over her face. "Better than anything in the world," she said.

"Ever think about them?" asked her friend, her own face whitening as she spoke. "Think about their lovely little soft helplessness—when you hold them in your arms and have to do *everything* for them. Have to go and turn them over—see that the little ear isn't crumpled—that the covers are all right. Can't you see 'em, upside down on the bath apron, grabbing at things, perfectly happy, but prepared to howl when it comes to dressing? And when they are big enough to love you! Little soft arms that will hardly go round your neck. Little soft cheeks against yours, little soft mouths and little soft kisses,—ever think of them?"

The girl's eyes were like stars. She was looking into the future; her breath came quickly; she sat quite still.

The doctor swallowed hard, and went on. "We mostly don't go much farther than that at first. It's just the babies we want. But you can look farther—can follow up, year by year, the lovely

changing growing bodies and minds, the confidence and love
between you, the pride you have as health is established, strength
and skill developed, and character unfolds and deepens.

"Then when they are grown, and sort of catch up, and you
have those splendid young lives about you, intimate strong friends
and tender lovers. And you feel as though you had indeed done
something for the world."

She stopped, saying no more for a little, watching the girl's
awed shining face. Suddenly that face was turned to her, full of
exquisite sympathy, the dark eyes swimming with sudden tears; and
two soft eager arms held her close.

"Oh, Doctor! To care like that and not—!"

"Yes, my dear;" said the doctor, quietly. "And not have any.
Not be able to have any—ever."

Vivian caught her breath with pitying intensity, but her
friend went on.

"Never be able to have a child, because I married a man
who had gonorrhea. In place of happy love, lonely pain. In place
of motherhood, disease. Misery and shame, child. Medicine and
surgery, and never any possibility of any child for me."

The girl was pale with horror. "I—I didn't know—" She tried
to say something, but the doctor burst out impatiently:

"No! You don't know. I didn't know. Girls aren't taught a
word of what's before them till it's too late—not *then*, sometimes!
Women lose every joy in life, every hope, every capacity for service
or pleasure. They go down to their graves without anyone's telling
them the cause of it all."

"That was why you—left him?" asked Vivian presently.

"Yes, I left him. When I found I could not be a mother I
determined to be a doctor, and save other women, if I could."

She said this with such slow, grave emphasis that Vivian turned a sudden startled face to her, and went white to the lips.

"I may be wrong," the doctor said, "you have not given me your confidence in this matter. But it is better, a thousand times better, that I should make this mistake than for you to make that. You must not marry Morton Elder."

Vivian did not admit nor deny. She still wore that look of horror. "You think he has—That?"

"I do not know whether he has gonorrhea or not; it takes a long microscopic analysis to be sure; but there is every practical assurance that he's had it, and I know he's had syphilis."

If Vivian could have turned paler she would have, then.

"I've heard of—that," she said, shuddering.

"Yes, the other is newer to our knowledge, far commoner, and really more dangerous. They are two of the most terrible diseases known to us; highly contagious, and in the case of syphilis, hereditary. Nearly three-quarters of the men have one or the other, or both."

But Vivian was not listening. Her face was buried in her hands. She crouched low in agonized weeping.

"Oh, come, come, my dear. Don't take it so hard. There's no harm done you see, it's not too late."

"Oh, it *is* too late! It is!" wailed the girl. "I have promised to marry him."

"I don't care if you were at the altar, child; you *haven't* married him, and you mustn't."

"I have given my word!" said the girl dully. She was thinking of Morton now. Of his handsome face, with its new expression of respectful tenderness; of all the hopes they had built together; of his life, so dependent upon hers for its higher interests.

She turned to the doctor, her lips quivering. "He *loves* me!" she said. "I—we—he says I am all that holds him up, that helps him to make a newer better life. And he has changed so—I can see it! He says he has loved me, really, since he was seventeen!"

The older sterner face did not relax.

"He told me he had—done wrong. He was honest about it. He said he wasn't—worthy."

"He isn't," said Dr. Bellair.

"But surely I owe some duty to him. He depends on me. And I have promised—"

The doctor grew grimmer. "Marriage is for motherhood," she said. "That is its initial purpose. I suppose you might deliberately forego motherhood, and undertake a sort of missionary relation to a man, but that is not marriage."

"He loves me," said the girl with gentle stubbornness. She saw Morton's eyes, as she had so often seen them lately; full of adoration and manly patience. She felt his hand, as she had felt it so often lately, holding hers, stealing about her waist, sometimes bringing her fingers to his lips for a strong slow kiss which she could not forget for hours.

She raised her head. A new wave of feeling swept over her. She saw a vista of self-sacrificing devotion, foregoing much, forgiving much, but rejoicing in the companionship of a noble life, a soul rebuilt, a love that was passionately grateful. Her eyes met those of her friend fairly. "And I love him!" she said.

"Will you tell that to your crippled children?" asked Dr. Bellair. "Will they understand it if they are idiots? Will they see it if they are blind? Will it satisfy you when they are dead?"

The girl shrank before her.

"You *shall* understand," said the doctor. This is no case for idealism and exalted emotion. Do you want a son like Theophile?"

"I thought you said—they didn't have any."

"Some don't—that is one result. Another result—of gonorrhea—is to have children born blind. Their eyes may be saved, with care. But it is not a motherly gift for one's babies—blindness. You may have years and years of suffering yourself—any or all of those diseases 'peculiar to women' as we used to call them! And we pitied the men who 'were so good to their invalid wives'! You may have any number of still-born children, year after year. And every little marred dead face would remind you that you allowed it! And they may be deformed and twisted, have all manner of terrible and loathsome afflictions, they and their children after them, if they have any. And many do! dear girl, don't you see that's wicked?"

Vivian was silent, her two hands wrung together; her whole form shivering with emotion.

"Don't think that you are 'ruining his life'," said the doctor kindly. "He ruined it long ago—poor boy!"

The girl turned quickly at the note of sympathy.

"They don't know either," her friend went on. "What could Miss Orella do, poor little saint, to protect a lively young fellow like that! All they have in their scatter-brained heads is 'it's naughty but it's nice!' And so they rush off and ruin their whole lives—and their wives'—and their children's. A man don't have to be so very wicked, either, understand. Just one mis-step may be enough for infection."

"Even if it did break his heart, and yours—even if you both lived single, he because it is the only decent thing he can do now, you because of a misguided sense of devotion; that would be better than to commit this plain sin. Beware of a biological sin, my dear; for it there is no forgiveness."

She waited a moment and went on, as firmly and steadily as she would have held the walls of a wound while she placed the stitches.

"If you two love each other so nobly and devotedly that it is higher and truer and more lasting than the ordinary love of men and women, you might be 'true' to one another for a lifetime, you see. And all that friendship can do, exalted influence, noble inspiration—that is open to you."

Vivian's eyes were wide and shining. She saw a possible future, not wholly unbearable.

"Has he kissed you yet?" asked the doctor suddenly.

"No," she said. "That is—except—"

"Don't let him. You might catch it. Your friendship must be distant. Well, shall we be going back? I'm sorry, my dear. I did hate awfully to do it. But I hated worse to see you go down those awful steps from which there is no returning."

"Yes," said Vivian. "Thank you. Won't you go on, please? I'll come later."

An hour the girl sat there, with the clear blue sky above her, the soft steady wind rustling the leaves, the little birds that hopped and pecked and flirted their tails so near her motionless figure.

She thought and thought, and through all the tumult of ideas it grew clearer to her that the doctor was right. She might sacrifice herself. She had no right to sacrifice her children.

A feeling of unreasoning horror at this sudden outlook into a field of unknown evil was met by her clear perception that if she was old enough to marry, to be a mother, she was surely old enough to know these things; and not only so, but ought to know them.

Shy, sensitive, delicate in feeling as the girl was, she had a fair and reasoning mind.

The Vintage[1]

Charlotte Perkins Gilman

This is not a short story. It stretches out for generations. Its beginning was thousands of years ago, and its end is not yet in sight. Here we have only a glimpse, a cross section, touching sharply on a few lives.

There was a girl, in one of our proudest Southern states, a girl of good family, and very proud of it. She wore a string of family names—Leslie Vauremont Barrington Montroy. There were more names, which they followed back for centuries, still with pride, but they could not put them all on one girl.

One other thing she was proud of, her blazing health. A big, vigorous girl, she was, smooth skinned, firm muscled, athletic, tireless, with the steady cheerfulness and courageous outlook which rest so largely on good health. Otherwise, not proud at all, a gentle, wholesome loving woman, loyal and tender.

She had lovers a plenty, among them two, who seemed to stand an even chance; one was Howard Faulkner, a young doctor, a friend, a neighbor, playmate from childhood; the other Rodger Moore, a college classmate and chum of the doctor, who had bought an estate next to the Montroys.

---

[1] Originally published in the October 1916 issue of *The Forerunner*.

Moore was rich, but that did not weigh with Leslie. Faulkner had enough, and for that matter she would have married a gypsy, if she had loved him—and followed him to the world's end.

She chose Moore.

Faulkner suffered, but bore it well. He had known Leslie so long, he was so genuinely fond of her, that he cared enough for her happiness to wish for it even above his own. It was hard to listen to Moore, though, but he did not wish to tell him of his own hurt. And it was hard to watch them together, to see her round and well-tanned arms driving the canoe through the shaded reaches of the level winding river, with Moore treated as a mere student of the art of paddling—till she divined that he did not quite like that role, and let him do it, though he was not nearly so proficient.

At tennis, he beat her, he had had far more practice, and with sterner opponents, but her swiftness and strength of arm gave him an enjoyable game, none the less, and it was a joy to the eye to see her boyish delight in it.

She could outdance him easily and outride him, too, having been used to the saddle from childhood, and to the wild, wide country for many miles around. In the water she could distance him again, and seemed a triumphant glittering nymph as she swept smiling through the sunlit ripples.

Everywhere she carried the joy of her splendid vigor, the beauty of abounding health.

Howard Faulkner was glad for her, and glad for his friend.

Moore was tremendously in love. He had loved before, as he frankly admitted even though she did not ask him, but it was "as moonlight is to sunlight and as water is to wine" he told her. "Men are men—and women are women, you see. I was no different from other men. But you—you are different. You are like—it sounds cheap to say a goddess, but that's what I always think of, that victory thing—but all there—and so beautiful! I've never known a woman like you—within a thousand miles of you. You make me think of snow and wind and sunshine and pine trees; you're so *clean!* You are the kind of woman a man can worship."

She was, and he did. He was no poet, his praises were not novel, but he loved her with all his heart,—and body.

The day was set for the wedding.

Then a slight throat affection annoyed him. He took it to Dr. Faulkner and Faulkner's face went white. He asked a few necessary questions, but Moore saw the drift, and scouted the idea.

"Nonsense, Howard," he said. "That was years and years ago. I was entirely cured. Don't for heaven's sake, revive that bugaboo *now.*"

"Now is exactly when you must face it, Rodger," said his friend. "I'm sorry. I don't know anything more dreadful to tell a man, but you were not cured. You have syphilis in your system. You know the result—it is communicable—and inheritable. You cannot marry—not for years, nor till after the most thorough proof that it is gone."

Moore was as pale as the other, now, and as firm. "I don't doubt your doing your duty, Howard, as you see it; but I tell you it's absurd. I've had the best treatment; I was thoroughly cured, I tell you."

"You can go through the tests again," Faulkner urged. "You can at least wait—the risk is too terrible for you to take—to let another take."

"It would be if there was any," said Moore doggedly. "You've got the thing on the brain, Howard. Talk about waiting!—with the invitations out and all of the county coming. What should I tell them, pray?"

"You can make some excuse, you can go to her father."

Moore laughed briefly. "Yes, and say good-bye. I will not have my life's happiness thwarted by one man's opinion, not while I have the verdict of certainly as good physicians on my side."

He was a determined man. This brief black incident in his past had long since been buried by that strong will, and he would not allow it to rise now like a skeleton at the feast.

Understand—he did not really in cold blood decide to offer such a risk to the women he loved. He refused to admit that there was a risk. And Faulkner? He was sure of his opinion but could not prove it without tests to which Moore would not submit; without time, which Moore would not allow.

He urged, he fairly begged, he used every argument and appeal he could think of to his friend, with the result that Moore would not come near him.

What else could he do? He was a physician with a high sense of professional honor. The physician must not betray his patient....

So he held his tongue, and saw the woman he had loved so long, all white and radiant in her bridal glory, marry the man with the worst of communicable diseases.

The first baby was a boy. A boy who soon looked out on life with his mother's eyes, large, clear, truthful, brave, loving. A boy of marked intelligence, affectionate, devoted to both his adoring parents. A boy who was a hopeless cripple.

Leslie could not believe it.

She had borne strange ailments, unlooked-for distress, supposing it to be part of her condition; supporting herself always by her happiness with her husband, and with hope; murmuring to herself "and when the child came, lovely as a star"—

He came—not lovely to look at, but for all that a joy to her maternal heart.

The next one died at birth; and better so.

The next one never lived to be born.

Again and again she undertook the mother task, to mould and fashion with long love and patience another child; again and again illness and premature failure.

And the father, a man strong in his domestic feelings, worshipping his wife, idolizing the one frail little son who followed him about so lovingly, longing for other children who should grow to be strong men like himself, beautiful women like their mother— what did he feel? As the little blasted buds came and went, without even breathing, what did their father feel?

As a husband, too, as a lover, more of a lover rather than less, as years showed more clearly the sweet and noble character of his wife, what did he feel to watch the proud clean beauty of the woman he adored wither and disappear.

He had to watch it. He had to comfort her as he could, with every tenderness, every devotion, as her health weakened, her beauty fled from her, and the unmistakable ravages of the disease began to show.

She did not know what was the matter with her, or with her children. She never had known that there was such a danger before "a decent woman," though aware of some dark horror connected with "sin," impossible even to mention.

Her old family physician told her nothing—that was not his place.

Her minister told her that her affliction was "the will of God."

It is astonishing what a low opinion of God some people hold.

Leslie bore up bravely for her husband's sake, for her child's. That little crooked body, how she loved and tended it. That sweet young spirit, what a constant joy it was.

And her husband she idolized. His gentleness, his devotion, his endless patience, his continued tender admiration long after her relentless mirror told her that she was no longer pleasant to look at, even after she wore a veil when going out—these made her cling to him with adoring grateful love.

"You are so good to me, Rodger, dear!" she breathed, when the merciful darkness covered her face. "I never dreamed a man could be so good to a woman!"

A shudder shook him.

"I am not good, Leslie," he said with rigid quietness. "But I love you. God! How I love you!"

He did. He had from the beginning. The more she suffered, the more he loved her. The more he loved her, the more he suffered. It lasted for years.

When she was taken away in the prime of her womanhood by "the inscrutable Will Above," as the white-headed minister phrased it, Rodger was almost glad. He was glad, wholly glad, for her.

For a beautiful and vigorous young woman to see a slow repulsive disease gradually overwhelm her is a misery the end of which deserves gratitude.

Her absolute, exquisite love had been his, and he had done all that lay in his power to make her life bearable.

Her last words to him were: "You have made me happy, Rodger,—so happy! I—love—you...."

Dr. Faulkner attended the funeral.

Father and son were inseparable. Rodger turned to that pathetic child, little Leslie (they had decided that, boy or girl, the child should bear that family name), with the grim determination that in so far as his life could serve, it should go to make up to the boy for his loss—his bitter loss and pain.

There was money enough.

There was the fine old place with all its freedom and beauty.

There was the subtlest, wisest education, bringing to the opening mind the wonders and beauties of life, developing all its power. There was travel, too, as soon as the boy was old enough to enjoy it; they went far and wide together, learning what the world was like.

There was music, too, unnumbered books, great pictures.

There was everything except companionship of his own age. He shrank from other boys, or perhaps they shrank from him. And he was so deeply content in his father's society that he seemed to miss nothing.

Together they went everywhere, together they stayed happily at home. As his father had been a playmate in the nursery and in the years of childhood, so he remained a playmate and schoolmate, studying with him, bringing all his long-trained patience and concentration to bear with the ceaseless purpose—"I will make up to him as far as I can. I will!"

Once, when the boy was about twelve years old, a small, weazened child, with the large beautiful head set low on the crooked shoulders, he sat in his father's arms one evening, in the big chair before the fire.

The large, rich room was very quiet; the red blaze held their eyes. They held each other close and were silent.

Then the child looked up into the man's eyes and asked soberly, "Father—why did God make me like this?"....

As he grew older, he grew stronger.

His face and head were of marked beauty, his eyes always the eyes of his mother.

He was a brilliant boy. With the help of tutors, he took a college course at home, his father always freshly interested.

"It's no use my going to college," said Leslie. "Colleges are for athletes, not students, as far as I can see. And I don't like the way the boys talk—from what I read of it."

So he lived with his father on the old place, in a companionship that grew with the years, and the boy was happy. His father watched him with ceaseless care, and so far as he could see, the boy was happy.

"If I can keep him so!" he murmured through set teeth. "No woman will love him—I must make up to him for everything."

For the boy's sake he kept himself young. He took unremitting care of his health.

"I must live," he said. "I shall live as long as he does, poor lad—perhaps. At any rate I must live as long as possible and be as strong as possible, for his sake."

So the man, who would gladly have died long since, set himself in all ways to preserve his health and remain with his son.

There came to the neighborhood for a summer's vacation a tall, sweet-faced girl, not at all like those Leslie had met, a woman, not a child. She had read as he had read. She had studied, was a college graduate, had traveled, too. More, she had worked as he had not. A little older than he, and of far wider experience, with a life of social enthusiasm and civic purpose.

She met the shy boy on a forest walk, and cheerfully made friends with him, taking the nettle firmly in both hands as it were.

"You feel badly because you are not like other folks," she said; "bless you, that's nothing to some of my friends, and they are jolly boys, too."

And she told him of this one and that one who bore worse physical disabilities by far, who had none of his compensating advantages, and who just went about their business like other people—"as far as they can, that is."

They became great friends. His father watched it with pleasure.

"He needs someone besides me," he thought, though there was a little jealous pain he would not admit. "She's a nice woman, a lady and all that, and her Settlement work and so on will interest him."

So they met often, and young Leslie grew more of a man, visibly, from the fresh experience she brought to him, the new friends she introduced, the new lines of reading opened to his eager interest.

Through her he began to see the world, not as his father had always regarded it, as a place of other people and somewhere else, but as the place where he really lived, his own place, with duties, powers and responsibilities.

With her he somehow felt strong, straight, like other men. She did not seem to mind deformity. And then, in spite of himself, unexpectedly, irresistibly, he found that he loved her....

This pain he took to his father, dumbly. "Take me away," he begged. "Let us go somewhere, anywhere. I love her, father! Such a thing as I have dared to love a woman! Let us go away, quickly."

His son must bear this, too; must love as men love; yet not even ask for happiness; he must suffer, and his father must see him bear it. This he had never looked for. The woman was a few years older, was not beautiful—but it had come. So they made preparations for a journey, a long one, far across the world.

But they met again in the forest paths, and had a clear talk. Leslie came to his father with shining eyes, walking as on air.

"She loves me, Father!" he said. "A woman loves me—loves me! She does not mind—she has made me feel that it does not matter. Oh—Father—she has lifted the load that has weighed on me since first I knew I was—different. It is gone, all gone, because it does not exist for her!

"Think, Father, think what it means. I can live in the world and work, do a real man's work. She says I can do more than many, that I am needed. Love, Father, for me, a home of my own,—reverent, his eyes bright with happy Even, perhaps," his face grew grave and tears—"a little boy of my own, some day, to love as you have loved me."

And his father saw how all his days and nights of ceaseless devotion had in no way made up to the boy for losing the common things of life. He saw how this unhoped-for happiness had come like water to the desert and filled his barren life with flowers. He saw what it meant to his boy he so loved, to have the door so open to him.

And he his father, had to tell his son that he must never marry—and why....

After a while the boy spoke, in a strange dead voice.

"All my little brothers and sisters? was that—?"

"Yes" said the miserable man.

"And—my mother?"....

He nodded; he could not speak.

The boy stood still looking at the man, whose carefully fostered strength seemed all to have left him in an hour, and the resistless years to have swept down upon him like a flood of iron.

He came to him with a low cry—.

"Oh my poor father!"

Annie Nathan Meyer was born in New York City on February 19, 1867, to a Sephardic Jewish family. The youngest daughter of Annie Florence Nathan (d. 1878) and Robert Weeks Nathan (d. 1888), Meyer was born to privilege. The Nathans were prominent members of the community and especially the New York City elite. Historians often remember Meyer for her role in founding Barnard College, one of the Seven Sisters institutions that was among the first to grant women college degrees. However, she was also a prolific writer. During her career, Meyer wrote no less than thirty plays; sixty-three short stories, essays, and sketches published in periodicals; three novels; three memoirs (including an autobiography); three non-fiction guides, including *My Park Book* and *The Gallery-Goers Book;* and an edited collection of feminist essays entitled *Women's Work in America.*

CPSIA information can be obtained
at www.ICGtesting.com
Printed in the USA
LVHW031628300321
682969LV00004B/1000

9 781942 885580